Lightning
and Blackberries

Joanne K. Jefferson

NIMBUS
PUBLISHING

Nimbus Publishing Limited
PO Box 9166, Halifax, NS B3K 5M8
(902) 455-4286 www.nimbus.ca

Printed and bound in Canada
Nimbus Publishing is committed to protecting our natural environment. As part of our efforts, this book is printed on 100% recycled content, Enviro 100.
Cover design: Cathy MacLean
Interior design: Margaret Issenman
Author photo: J. Shields

This novel is a work of fiction. Names, characters, places, and incidents are either the product of the author's imagination or are used fictitiously. Any resemblance to actual persons, living or dead, events or locales is entirely coincidental.

Library and Archives Canada Cataloguing in Publication

Jefferson, Joanne K. (Joanne Kent), 1963-
Lightning and blackberries / Joanne Jefferson.
ISBN 978-1-55109-654-4
I. Title.
PS8619.E44L44 2008   jC813'.6   C2008-900403-5

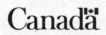  

We acknowledge the financial support of the Government of Canada through the Book Publishing Industry Development Program (BPIDP) and the Canada Council, and of the Province of Nova Scotia through the Department of Tourism, Culture and Heritage for our publishing activities.

Acknowledgements

I am grateful to my father, Stephen Evans Jefferson, and his brother, Philip, for inspiring me with family history.

Thanks to the Oxford Street Writers' Group for ten years of feedback and encouragement, Sandra McIntyre and everyone at Nimbus, mentors Joan Clark and Julie Johnston, and the Writers' Federation of Nova Scotia.

To Paul, Thomas, Will and the rest of the family, I appreciate your faithful support.

Evans Hall, Annapolis
March 1794

My Dearest Abigail,

I know you are about to pass your eighteenth birthday and in honour of that occasion I am sending you a small gift. My mother gave this book to me twenty years ago, when I turned eighteen. I want you to have it.

If you choose to read what I wrote in these pages, you will learn how I became connected to someone who changed my life.

I hope the arrival of your first baby is easy and peaceful. As a wife of two years already you are possessed of experience and wisdom I did not have at your age. I wish you all future happiness.

Give my love to everyone.

Chapter One

"*B*etsy! Betsy!" The rough wind carried Sadie's voice across the yard. She was using my short name, though I had asked her many times to give it up. In better weather I would have been farther away, by the brook, or on the marsh, but early March allowed no wandering and Sadie's demands had to be answered.

"She'll probably tell me I've been acting like a child and should be called by a child's name," I said to Hazel as she munched the last apple from my pocket. I pressed my face against her neck, feeling the thick toughness of the winter coat she wore. I felt like I was covered in a thick layer of dust that was slowly smothering me. After so many dull, dark weeks indoors full of talk and sewing I just wanted to shake off winter the way Hazel shook the flies away.

"Don't fret," I told her as I latched the stall. "You'll be having green grass again soon enough."

I crossed the yard with wet snowflakes clinging to my shawl, clumped together in lumpy shapes that were nothing like the delicate creations that had fallen in the cold days of January. There was a heavy, raw dampness in the air.

Inside, the kitchen was warm and Sadie was taking cornbread out of the pan. "Your company's waiting in the front room," she said without looking up from her work.

I helped myself to a corner of the bread and ate it carefully so as not to burn my tongue. "Sadie, don't you think seventeen's a bit old to be called by a child's name?"

"I'd say it's a lot too old to be hiding in the barn. And brush the hay off yourself. You'll scare the poor girl half to death. She'll be thinking you're some wild creature that never saw the inside of a house. Now, go on."

I laughed, but smoothed my clothes a little as I made my way from the kitchen to the sitting room. The looking glass in the hall showed me wisps of escaping hair around a freckled face. A good strong face, I told my reflection. I was glad to have my father's eyebrows.

"Well, Elizabeth, finally." Mother's cheeks were spotted pink, betraying her impatience. She was sitting in one of her matching chairs with the plum-coloured upholstery. They had come from her family home. I was allowed to sit on one only if Mother first inspected my hands and my skirts. Nothing from the barn could touch her precious chairs.

"Hello, Mother," I said. "Hello, Charlotte. I'm sorry you had to wait." Charlotte Rice came once a week with the hope that I could teach her to play the piano. Her father had arranged the lessons. Since Mrs. Rice had died, he'd explained, Charlotte needed female companionship and instruction. I was dreading the day when Mother would decide that the widowed Mr. Rice would make a good husband and I a suitable new mother for Charlotte, even though she was only three years younger.

Charlotte rose to her feet. "Hello, Miss Elizabeth. I don't mind a bit. Mrs. Evans and I have been catching up."

Mother smiled then, a wistful smile, reminding me that Charlotte was the kind of girl she would have liked me to be. A girl who wanted to play the piano because she knew ladies should have accomplishments. A girl who wore clothes that were always clean and neat, no matter what the weather. A girl who liked sitting rooms more than kitchens or barns.

"I'll leave you alone to your lessons," Mother said, getting up from the chair and then, as she always did, patting her chest as if to propel air into her fragile lungs. "I feel the need for a rest. Your father is coming from town this afternoon, Elizabeth. I certainly hope you'll put on your corset before supper."

I felt my shoulders tighten. "Yes, Mother." As she was leaving the room I rolled my eyes and gritted my teeth so Charlotte could see. She hid her giggle behind one small hand.

"Oh, Miss Elizabeth, I do love coming to your house," Charlotte said as we took the sheets of music from the cupboard. "I don't know of a more beautiful place than Evans Hall. And when I think that your father designed it. My father is only good at writing sermons, not building grand houses."

"Mother is always complaining about the drafts," I told her, "and the dreadful wilderness." I did my best imitation of Mother's disgust. "Of course, she says the houses she was used to in Massachusetts would put this one to shame. She always talks about the estates that line the post road from Boston to Sudbury and how she and her sisters attended parties in more than half of them."

"Oh, imagine it," Charlotte said. "Being in the ballroom of one of those enormous homes, everyone dressed in the latest fashions, the officers so handsome in uniforms…" She carefully arranged the folds of her skirt as she sat at the piano.

"Sounds hideous, if you ask me." I shuddered at the thought of too-tight, itchy dresses and fussy hair ribbons.

Charlotte allowed her giggle to escape this time. "May I begin with the waltz I've been practising?"

I nodded and closed my eyes to listen. Even if she and I disagree on what makes for a good daydream, I thought, at least she doesn't judge me unfairly.

After Charlotte had gone, I went back to the kitchen and sat at the table peeling turnips and watching the snowflakes drift past the window. Sadie moved about the kitchen, busy with the biscuits, and the salt pork, and the pie. I knew Mother often felt overwhelmed by the smells and noise of the kitchen. I pitied her. I found it to be one of the most peaceful spots in the house.

Soon I heard Father's footsteps in the hall and listened for the other familiar sounds—the flap of his cloak as he shook off the melted snow, Mother's slow step on the stair, and the murmuring of their conversation. When he came into the kitchen, he gave me a cool kiss on the cheek. Drops of icy water fell from his wig.

"It's good to be back at home." He sat down by the fire, holding his hands toward its generous warmth.

He'd been away in Annapolis Royal for several days while court was in session. I was proud of Father for his work as a judge, colonel of the militia, and township treasurer, but I wished it didn't keep him away from the farm so much.

"Your mother's still feeling poorly, I gather."

"She was upstairs most of the afternoon," I told him.

Sadie snorted. "She's lonesome. That's all. Cooped up in this nasty weather, no company—she's out of sorts." She took the lantern off the mantel. "I'm going down to the cellar for some apples."

After she disappeared through the narrow doorway we could hear her thumping her way slowly down the stairs. No one else understood Mother the way Sadie did. She had been a slave in the Sudbury house from the time they were both little girls and had helped Mother through all her sorrows since they had left New England.

Father cleared his throat. "I have some news," he said. I went on peeling, expecting a courthouse tale. "Some time ago I posted an advertisement for a farm assistant, and I've had a reply from a young man in Yorkshire who's looking for a position. He'll be coming over this spring, in time for planting."

I stared at him, surprised out of words, with a piece of turnip in one hand and the knife in the other.

Father sighed. "I've given you an unpleasant shock, haven't I?"

An angry string of protests came bubbling out of me as I felt a hot flush radiating from my neck and cheeks. "Why do we need someone to help with the farm? Sadie and I do our part and you've always had the neighbours' help in the busy times. Why ask a stranger to come and live here?" I chopped randomly at the turnips, feeling the sharp crack of the knife against the board. "Why didn't you tell me you were thinking of this? Why wait until you had found someone?"

"I didn't want to have everyone in an uproar until I knew for certain he would be coming. Elizabeth, you must remember that I am no longer a young and energetic man." This was Father's speech-making tone. I knew it well. He had obviously practised his answers carefully. "I had great dreams for this place. I planned to have fifty head of cattle by now." He sighed and rubbed his forehead. "I am still called upon to design buildings," he continued, "I have my duties as judge, and if I am elected to the Assembly I will have to spend much more time in Halifax. I cannot carry out those responsibilities and manage the planting and harvesting of the crops and tending of the animals. It is too much for one man. So I've gone looking for help. It's the only thing to do, apart from selling the farm."

"Selling the farm?" I felt as if the cold, musty air from the cellar was suddenly swirling around me. Goosebumps stood up on my arms. "You can't!" I looked at him, desperate for reassurance, but he was looking into the fireplace, deliberately avoiding my gaze.

The turnip pieces were already smaller than necessary, so I put down the knife and scooped them into my apron. Father sat silent as I went to the fire and let my burden fall into the pot. Water splashed and hissed against the hot bricks. I stared into the pulsating coals, trying to slow my heartbeat.

"What is his name?"

"Jefferson. Robert Jefferson. He comes from a village called Bielby."

"And why isn't he getting a land grant and starting up his own farm?"

"I imagine he wants a chance to see what is here, to learn something about the prospects before making a decision to stay."

"I see."

Father leaned back and closed his eyes. "Just this morning I received his letter agreeing to my terms. I'm sure we'll find him suitable, my dear."

"Well, he best not try to tell me how to milk my cows, or interfere with our garden." I looked out the window, knowing that the catch in my voice would turn to tears if I looked at Father's face. The light from the house shone yellow through the falling snow.

"No, of course he will not." Father stood and stretched. "I have some papers to sort out in my study. Call for me when supper is ready, will you please?"

Sadie emerged from the cellar and plunked the basket

of apples on the table. "I'm glad to hear your father's finally doing the sensible thing," she said.

"He could at least have asked for my opinion." I knew, in the clear light of reason, that Father's decision was the right one, especially if the alternative was losing the farm. But my heart was having trouble accepting the notion of an outsider occupying part of our house, working in our fields, taking over. I wanted the farm to be ours, just as it always had been.

"He's thinking ahead to your marriage."

"Don't be ridiculous." I gathered up the turnip peelings and tossed them into the scrap basket for the pig.

"It'll happen sooner rather than later, Betsy. Before long you'll be planting your garden and weaving your linen at your husband's house. Some nice fellow from over in Granville, maybe, or upriver." She got up from the chair and began taking plates off the shelf of the cabinet, handing them to me to put around the table.

"I'll not be doing any such thing."

"Oh, so you'll go with your mother to Sudbury to find a husband? A Yankee?" She had a big smile on her face.

"I said it before and I'll say it again. I'll stay right here and be a farmer for the rest of my life. I don't need a husband for that." I banged the last plate at Father's place.

"Good thing that's pewter, miss. You'd be in serious trouble for smashing the china." We worked in silence for a while and I thought the conversation was over until she spoke again. This time she wasn't teasing. "You think being your father's only child means you don't need a husband to make a place for yourself, but there's more to it than that. A woman alone doesn't have much of a life."

"What about all those widows who carry on farming after their husbands are gone? Like Mrs. Spurr."

"Yes, and look at those sturdy sons she's got out behind her oxen. She didn't grow those in the garden, now did she?"

"Ooh." I growled with frustration. Sometimes it was impossible to argue with Sadie. I reached to move the boiling turnips away from the coals and my face felt so hot with anger that the nearness of the fire made no impression.

Father coaxed Mother into coming down for supper and as we finished off the apple pie at suppertime, he surprised us with another bit of news.

"I nearly forgot," he said, winking at me as he reached into his waistcoat pocket, "I've had a letter from Sudbury."

"Henry!" Mother tried to seize it, but Father held it away. She scolded him. "How could you forget such a thing? What does it say?"

"Well, let me see…" Father put on his glasses and scanned the letter. "There is some comment about the state of things in Massachusetts. Where is it now…oh, yes. 'Our political affairs are in confusion, no tea to be drank but all sunk in the sea as soon as it arrives in our harbour.' Imagine, the nerve of that rebellious lot. And I'll wager your brother agrees with them."

"Henry." Mother had no patience for politics and was now perched on the edge of her chair, her face full of colour for the first time in days. "What of the family? How is Abigail? And Lydia?" She was always desperate for news of her sisters.

"Well, I think there was some mention of a baby."

She snatched the letter from him and began to read with a little frown, and then a cry of delight. "Oh, my word, Lydia's had a boy. Now Henry, why would you pass over that part? How dare you? And his name is Seth. Where in heaven did they find a name like that?"

She read on in silence, moving her lips a little from time to time. When she was finished she let the pages rest in her lap with a heavy sigh. I knew she would carry them with her for at least a week, reading and rereading, laughing one minute and crying the next, until they were damp and wrinkled. I could never decide if her attachment to the past was a blessing or a curse.

Chapter Two

A few days later, after an overnight snowfall had left the world glittering and clean, Father came to the breakfast table with a smile on his face. "I'm going out to check the snares this morning," he said as I handed him a cup of tea. "I could use your help."

I nodded and hurried to finish my breakfast. Few things were more satisfying to me than working outdoors on such a day. Sadie acted like she was offended at being left with the chores, but I noticed her smile as she handed me my mittens and the satchel. She would probably rather be rid of me than listen to my complaints about being stuck indoors. I had wound four skeins of wool the evening before and knew she would spend much of the morning at the loom.

"Don't be late for dinner," she said.

The air was crisp and the sun dazzling on the smooth expanses of snow all around the house. It was the best of winter weather; one last gift before the thaw began. We headed out across the back pasture toward the edge of the woods, our snowshoes kicking up showers of powder. We were halfway across the open field when Father turned to look at the valley below us. The river was a dark ribbon weaving through blank, white fields.

"Elizabeth, my dear, I think I might go mad if I couldn't see this view whenever I needed to. Sometimes when I'm in Halifax, among the buildings and streets and the rush of people, I think of the valley and our farm and my spirit settles. Even if I can't see it with my eyes, my heart knows it well enough. But there's nothing quite like being here, especially on a glorious day like this."

"If you asked Mother, she would say she hated it. How can you and she be so different and yet be married?"

"Married people usually are different. That's the difficulty. But it can also be the strength, the balance. Like the valley and the mountain." He pointed across to the dark ridge at the horizon. "One wouldn't exist without the other."

Sadie's words about marriage leaped into my mind, and I turned my attention to walking again in an effort to escape them. It was too fine a day for dark thoughts about the future. I took several long strides before something in the snow made me stop again. It was a set of tracks, small footprints made by a tiny creature. Probably a field mouse, I thought. I followed the marks with my eye for a moment, then saw where feathers had brushed the snow and talons had pierced its surface.

Father crouched beside me. "Look how far apart the wingtips are." His outstretched arms fell short in comparison.

"The mouse got away." I pointed to the reappearance of the tiny tracks.

"He probably dove under the snow just as the bird was striking."

We walked on, admiring the agility of the escaping mouse and the persistence of the bird. And then we came to the spot where the snow had been completely disturbed by the wings and talons and body all touching at once.

"Poor mouse," I said. "I suppose it was an owl that got him."

"It would take a lot more than one mouse to satisfy that predator," Father said, and we continued on our trek toward the dark trees.

In the snares, which were set along a well-used rabbit path, we found two still bodies, their paws stretched out, their noses quiet. I let my hand rest in the soft fur as I removed the lines. I hoped they had died easily and knew they'd make a fine stew for a late winter supper.

On the way back to the house, Father said, "Have your feelings about the hired man changed at all?"

"Well…I don't like to admit it but I am curious." It seemed easier now to think about the stranger who was coming. Having more help with the farm might allow Father to spend more time with me. "Do you know anything else about him? Does he have family in Yorkshire? Why does he want to leave?"

Father laughed. "All I can tell you is that his family has been farming, but rents are high and there's little hope for prosperity where he is."

"Does Mother know?"

"I'll tell her tonight, after supper. I needed your approval first."

Those few words made me feel even happier. I was still Father's second-in-command on the farm. I scooped up some snow and tossed it at him, catching him by surprise, full in the face. He came back at me with his own handful of white, but I ducked away and set out running for home.

My tasks for the afternoon included a pile of mending. I wanted to continue the morning's companionship, so I took my work to Father's study where I found him dozing beside the fire. His gleaming sword hung above the mantel, the book spines stood straight on their shelves, the rolled drawings were upright in their holder. The room was as comforting as ever.

I sat near him on the little footstool where the warmth of the flames would reach me. As the needle poked up and down in rhythm with Father's snores, I thought about all the afternoons I'd spent in that room, struggling over lessons in history, or French. Father would open the grammar book and I would groan and complain about irregular verbs, and try my best to divert him.

"Why do you and Mother insist that I learn French?" I had asked one rainy afternoon when I was about twelve. "There are no French people here. What use could it possibly be?"

"It's good for the mind to learn another language," Father had replied. "It's what you would be studying if you had done as your mother wished and gone to school in Boston. But you're right, there are no French people here now, none to speak of. Those families who once lived here were offered a chance to stay if they would swear an oath of allegiance to the king. They refused and left the province."

"Where did they go?" I had rarely been satisfied with the simple answer.

"They went back to France." Father had begun to lose his patience then. "And now you must go back to conjugating verbs, miss."

Poor Father, I thought now. How I tested him. I looked up from my stitches to see that he was awake and watching me.

"What are you smiling about, Elizabeth?" He reached for his pipe and tapped it carefully against the hearth, then against the palm of his hand.

"French lessons."

"They certainly never brought a smile to your face before. You tried everything you could think of to wriggle out of them."

"I know. I was just remembering all the questions I asked about the French families who used to farm along the river."

"You were a regular pest about the subject." He was filling his pipe methodically.

"You never seemed very comfortable with those questions, Father. Perhaps that's why I kept digging. I knew I had found a subject that made you uneasy." I pulled at a thread that had come loose in the hem of my apron. Another mending project, I thought.

"I was trying to simplify a very complex situation in order to explain it to you." He held a taper in the coals, then brought the bright flame to the bowl of his pipe. I watched as it rose up between each of his drawing breaths. When the tobacco was lit to his satisfaction he shook out the flame. "Deporting the Acadians was more than a bit awkward for the government. No one was particularly easy with the notion of forcing people away from their homes."

I couldn't remember him using the word "force" before. My nose was tingling, irritated by the smoke. I stifled a sneeze and brought my needle back to where I had stopped.

"You weren't here when the Acadians left, were you?"

"No, I didn't arrive in Halifax until two years afterward. And it was another year before Governor Lawrence opened up the land for settlement."

"There's not much left of them now." I bit through the thread and tied it off. Not as tidy as Sadie's work, I thought, but it'll have to do.

"No," Father released another puff of smoke. "There are a few stone foundations over in Belle Isle, and more upriver, near Falmouth."

"And the dykes, of course." I knew my cows would be hungrier in winter without the sweet marsh hay we harvested every summer.

"They'll not last much longer, I'm afraid. All along the river, farmers are finding the dykes breaking apart and their fields flooding. One of these years we'll lose our own."

"Why not repair them?"

"The job would require far too much labour," he paused to tap the pipe against his palm. "With all the clearing that's being done we soon won't have a need for those soggy marshes and we won't have to waste our time figuring out how to keep them from flooding again."

"But surely someone knows how the dykes work. The Acadians obviously had the knowledge, and the ability to build them."

"Yes, but we are not them. In any case, my dear, it certainly won't be you out there hauling cartloads of sod and rock." He set aside his pipe and rose stiffly. "Now, I think it's time for a cup of tea, don't you?"

Later, I found Mother in the gloomy sitting room. "Are you feeling feverish again?" I asked.

"No, just weak, and my head aches."

"Do you need a cloth for your forehead? Some tea?" I wanted a task, some reason to avoid sitting down.

"No."

"I could read."

"I couldn't concentrate on that. Talk about something cheerful."

So I sat down and began to describe the lambs I'd seen at Mr. Lovett's farm the day before. They were newborns, still wobbly-legged and startled by the noise, the cold air, the touch of humans. I was planning to start my own herd and had already made a good bargain with Mr. Lovett for a ewe and two lambs.

Mother interrupted, "You waste far too much time out of doors and with the animals when you should be tending to your music and your needlework. If you had spent the last few years in a good Boston school instead of acting like a farmhand, I would not be so concerned for your future.

No husband wishes for a wife who would rather be picking berries and wandering the fields than tending to the proper refinement of the home. Do you understand?"

"Yes, Mother." I knew there was no other reply, though I wanted to shout at her that there was a lot more to farming than just picking berries and that I did not care about being a wife. I pressed my lips together to keep my tongue in check.

Mother burst out, "Why can't you confide in me, Elizabeth? Why can't you come to me with your dilemmas and ask for my advice and then we could discuss the answers together as mother and daughter should?"

I had no answer for her, only the familiar feeling of wanting to fly from the room as fast as I could. I gripped my leg to keep it from jiggling.

"I see Mrs. Perkins and her Anna together in church and I think to myself, now isn't that a pleasant sight, mother and daughter so close, so alike, almost like sisters, with their heads bent together. They have such affection for each other. Do you suppose people ever say the same thing about us?"

"I try not to wonder what others say about us, but if I did, I would hope that they would say I show respect for you."

"Oh, that is what is proper, but is it truthful? I know you wish you didn't have to keep me company—you'd rather be with Sadie, or your father, or your cows. Why, Elizabeth?

Why can't you feel for me the way I felt for my mother? Why?" She took her handkerchief from her sleeve and began dabbing at her eyes, sniffling.

For a moment I could only sit where I was, frozen. I wondered if there was some terrible fault in me that I did not rush to comfort her. Eventually, I moved to her side, taking her hand and stroking it. I maintained the pose for a long time, keeping in my mind the memory of Sadie doing the same for me when I was ill, or distraught. When Mother seemed calm, I walked out of the room without looking back. I didn't need to see her red-rimmed eyes, her melancholy expression.

The day's perfect snow quickly turned to grey slush. The following week we had a terrible sleet storm that iced the trees and coated the north windows with a second murky pane. By the next morning, though, the sky was soft and icicles began their pattering drip from the eaves before we had even begun preparing dinner.

I stepped outside the kitchen door and looked up into the hills behind the farm, turning my face toward the sun. My mind slipped easily into the relief of lighter clothing, of the early light, and lengthened evenings. Away with the candles and shoes, I thought. Let me feel the plow handles, the seed bag over my shoulder, the cool earth. Let me smell the apple blossoms when they fill the orchard with perfume.

I went back into the kitchen to face the morning's chores. Mr. and Mrs. Lovett were coming for supper and Sadie and I had much work to do. Even though the Lovetts were near neighbours and frequent visitors, their presence for a meal was an opportunity for Mother to impose her standards of civilization. She would never allow company to eat in the warm and cozy kitchen, so we had to light a fire in the dining room, polish up the silver, and get the china dishes from their cupboard. By the time I had done those chores, helped Sadie make soup and dumplings and raisin pudding, fetched the wine and beer from the cellar, laid out the good table linens, and washed the kitchen and hall floors, I was ready for a rest. Instead, anticipating Mother's insistence, I went to my room to pin up my hair and put on my corset.

As I started back down the stairs I paused, hearing my parents' voices below me. They were standing by the looking glass in the hall. Father was fastening the clasp on Mother's favourite pendant. I stayed hidden on the stairs, feeling like a small child again, not wanting to interrupt.

"Do you remember our first dinner party?" Father asked. "You were wearing this pendant that evening."

"Was that at the house in Boston? When the Governor was visiting?"

"Yes, and you insisted that the cook make the pies again since the crusts weren't as flaky as you liked."

"Well, a lady has to have standards. Besides, I'd get a bad reputation for serving second-rate pies at a state dinner." They both laughed, and then the Lovetts were at the door.

"Oh, Elizabeth," Mrs. Lovett gushed as I came down the stairs. "I swear you look prettier every time I see you!" She had kisses for everyone, as always. Her husband, as always, gave a silent nod of the head to Mother and me, and a terse "Colonel Evans" to Father. It wasn't until well into the meal, and the wine, that Mr. Lovett unbuttoned his coat and recounted the story he had been telling to me since I was young enough to sit on his knee.

"It's your father's fault I ever came here in the first place, you know," he said. "I was sure I would die on the voyage over. Sick as a dog, I was, and didn't recover till I'd been on solid ground for two days. I swore I'd never go to sea again, and I haven't. Even on my trips to Halifax I always go by land, no matter how bumpy the roads." Everyone laughed.

"And what is new in the Assembly chamber these days, Phineas?" Father said, leaning back in his chair.

"Now, gentlemen," Mother said before Mr. Lovett could launch into his inevitable long and boring account. "You know I'll have no talk of politics at my table. If you want to grumble about such things, you'll have to wait until after dessert. Ah, here's the pudding!"

Mrs. Lovett clapped her hands in delight as Sadie brought in the dessert. Father and Mr. Lovett followed Mother's wishes until after they had taken their glasses of port into the study. Once there, I knew, they would put their feet up and talk politics to their hearts' content. I, on the other hand, was obliged to sit in the front room with Mother and Mrs. Lovett.

"Give us a tune, Elizabeth," said Mrs. Lovett as she pulled her chair close to the card table.

"Yes, do, dear," Mother said, "but make it a cheerful tune, please." She began dealing out the cards. I sat at the piano and concentrated on my fingerings, letting the sound of the notes block out their gossip. They didn't pay much attention to the music, but at least they didn't make me join in the card game.

When the long evening was finally over, Mr. and Mrs. Lovett departed in a flurry of misplaced gloves and hats. Mrs. Lovett giggled like a girl when Father kissed her hand.

Mr. Lovett called over his shoulder on his way out the front door. "Find a husband for that daughter of yours soon, Evans!"

I retreated to the kitchen hoping Sadie had left some chores for me. Anything was better than listening to Mother's thoughts on that subject.

Chapter Three

The start of spring brought rain and ceaseless wind.

Once the skies cleared Sadie and I would begin our spring cleaning, but while it was still wet we passed the time sewing and weaving. The yard was all mud and it clumped on my shoes like badly cooked porridge, then dried in clods that dropped onto the floors where it crumbled to fine dust. In a few weeks, I reminded myself, I'd probably be complaining about my aching back as I tilled the same soil in preparation for planting the garden. By that time the hired man would have arrived and our house would no longer be our own.

I was deep in a dream in the darkest hour of a rainy morning when Sadie shook me out of sleep. I had been underwater, in the trout pool, and I had to struggle to the surface with Sadie's face above me.

"Betsy. Wake up. I need your help. It's Missus Spencer over by Sawmill Creek. Get dressed."

She gave me a mug of tea and a biscuit in the kitchen
and we headed out into the rain without speaking. It wasn't
often that she asked for my assistance with these missions
of hers, and she rarely spoke of all the women she'd helped.
She would have denied the title "midwife" but there wasn't a
woman in the township who wouldn't have benefited from
Sadie's hands when the pains came strong and heavy.

Sawmill Creek had become a raging torrent with the rain
and runoff, but Sadie and I found the bridge and crossed
safely. Inside the house Mrs. Spencer was on the bed in the
sitting room. Her daughter, about nine or ten years old, sat
beside the bed, pale and wide-eyed. I knew that Mr. Spencer
had been dead for only a few weeks, drowned when he fell
through the late winter ice.

As Sadie removed her wet cloak and began to empty her
bag, I glanced around the room. As in many small houses,
the sitting room served two purposes—sleeping space and
visiting space. It also, I judged, held their only significant
furniture: a chest, the chair, the bed, and a framed picture of
a lovely landscape with rolling hills and a stretch of water. A
boat with full sails was suspended in the centre of the picture,
never to reach the shore. Cows grazed on the hills.

Mrs. Spencer hollered with the pain and I turned from
the painting. Mercy, the oldest daughter, described to us

how her mother had begun having regular pains sometime
the previous day; but when she started screaming and there
was blood Mercy had sent her brother for the neighbour,
who rode to Evans Hall for Sadie. The baby, Sadie quickly
determined, was turned, one shoulder where its head should
have been. She spoke soothing words to Mrs. Spencer and
gave quick instructions to Mercy. The girl went upstairs
where I guessed the other children were waiting, scared and
cold, under the low, slanted ceiling of their room.

"John, John! Stay near me!" Mrs. Spencer cried out to her
dead husband. I almost looked over my shoulder, as if I might
see him standing in the doorway.

Sadie dripped beads of tincture into a cup. I held Mrs.
Spencer's perspiring head while Sadie held the cup to her
mouth. I thought of the hot days of August when I'd picked
the remedy's ingredients and helped Sadie hang them from
the kitchen ceiling to dry.

"The baby's got to turn," Sadie said, "or it'll not come out."

"It looks as if it's halfway out already."

"Shush." Sadie scowled.

My job was not to offer comment or suggestion, nor even
to ask questions. My part was to do as she told me and keep
quiet. I was an extra pair of hands, nothing more.

She began to press against the tiny shoulder, while at the

same time rubbing Mrs. Spencer's belly more vigorously
than I would have thought safe. It seemed to take forever,
but slowly, while Mrs. Spencer groaned and Sadie urged, the
baby's shoulder retreated, and slowly the enormous bulge
under the stretched skin changed shape.

Dawn brightened the sky outside the small windows.
Sometime during the morning I noticed that the rain had
let up, and I could see breaks in the lumpy clouds where blue
sky peeked through. I resisted the urge to run outside and
let the spring air clear my head. I wiped sweat from Mrs.
Spencer's face for the thousandth time and brought a cup of
tea from the kitchen for Sadie to gulp while she paused in
her work. Then I climbed the narrow stairs and found Mercy
surrounded by small children, all clutching the blankets and
staring at me.

"Don't be frightened," I said to them. "Sadie's good. She'll
help your mama. And look," I pointed to the window, "the
sun's coming out." Mercy pulled the blankets tighter around
her siblings and smiled bravely. They all jumped when
another sharp cry came up the stairs.

"Betsy!" Sadie's voice was urgent.

The baby was apparently tired of being confined and Mrs.
Spencer's body had decided to try again to force the infant
out. She groaned long and low, different sounds from the

agonized screams we'd heard when we first arrived. I held the stick for her to bite when the pushing started, and I kept her shoulders up off the bed. As the energy seemed to drain out of Mrs. Spencer with each round of effort, Sadie's face began to change. It looked like invisible strings were attached to her eyebrows, her cheeks, and the corners of her mouth. With each session of groaning and straining, those strings tightened and lifted Sadie's weary lines into a broad smile.

Finally, just as I thought Mrs. Spencer could do no more, there was a sudden gush and Sadie held up a tiny figure covered in a white coating and streaked with dark blood. We heard a croaking cry, and then Sadie separated the baby forever from his mother's body. When they touched each other again—the baby clean and wrapped and Mrs. Spencer miraculously still able to raise her arms—there was a moment of silence I knew I would never forget. Then the children pushed through the door and clamoured around their mother, all trying to touch the baby at once.

"Your mama needs quiet now," I told them after they'd had a peek. "Come on in the kitchen and we'll find some breakfast." I coaxed them from the sitting room and began the awkward process of finding food in the ill-stocked kitchen. There was some cheese, some potatoes, and a little dried meat. I wished I'd brought along a jug of milk. That would put roses on those pale cheeks again, I thought, and vowed that I would return with a fresh batch as soon as I could.

Sadie stayed to care for the baby while Mrs. Spencer slept, and I walked home alone. Picking my way along the muddy track, I breathed in the sweet spring air. The sky was bluer than it had been for months and I could almost see the buds fattening in the warm air. A robin burbled from high atop a birch, and I felt my heart expand with the freshness of it all. The world was new again.

As I walked up the lane toward Evans Hall I met Charlotte coming down.

"Oh, Charlotte, we were supposed to have a lesson this morning. I'm sorry." She looked so fresh in her pale blue dress and matching shawl, her shoes clean, her buckles sparkling, her stockings white. I was a mess—petticoat dragging through the mud, hair completely dishevelled, hands still red and raw from Sadie's strong soap. I explained to her where I'd been and her eyes widened, though whether in shock or admiration I was too sleepy to know. We agreed to meet later in the week.

Mother met me at the door. "Have you been out with Sadie all this time? Where is she? She knows I don't want her dragging you along on these escapades of hers. For heaven's sake, you shouldn't be seen as her helper. It isn't right. And besides, Charlotte was supposed to have a lesson this morning. She's just left, since you didn't have the courtesy to be here."

I didn't bother to argue with her, or explain. I was too tired, and too happy. Father had taken care of my cows, and the quilts on my bed were still thrown back from when I'd been awakened in the early hours. I fell into them and into a deep, satisfied sleep.

When I returned to the Spencer house that evening with a basket packed with cheese, butter, milk, bread, and two of our old quilts, Sadie was gathering her things. Mrs. Spencer sat on the edge of the bed with the baby nursing peacefully.

"Thank you," she said softly to Sadie as we were leaving. "I'll give you something when I can."

"Don't think of it," Sadie brushed away the woman's words. "You just take care. I'll come again in a day or so."

I knew that in a few weeks a package would arrive at Evans Hall for Sadie, some quiet gift that women like Mrs. Spencer always offered in return.

Chapter Four

On the fifth of May we observed our traditional spring fast, which meant a long dull day in church while the sunshine and warm breezes begged us to be outside. A week later we got word that Mr. Jefferson's ship, the *Thomas and William*, had arrived in Halifax and that he would travel to Annapolis as soon as he could arrange transport.

Mother decided the hired man should have Sadie's old room at the top of the back stairs. I thought we should make him sleep in the barn. Sadie was happy to move downstairs, next to the kitchen, since her knees had been giving her so much pain.

"You remember the morning I fell down those stairs?" she asked as we spread a quilt across the bed that was to be Mr. Jefferson's. "I'm sure I gave your father the scare of his life. Woke him right out of his sleep with my hollering."

"And broke your ankle too, right?"

"Yes. Couldn't do anything but sit by the fire for a month

or so. Haven't been so well-rested since." She shook her head, chuckling. I wondered if she was laughing at the memory of our pathetic attempts to manage without her.

I helped Sadie carry the last of her belongings downstairs, then went out to continue working on the sheep pen I was building beside the barn. It was a modest project, but it pleased me to make something new and sturdy with my own hands. I remembered the day Father had taken me to see Evans Hall under construction. It was not long after Mother and I had arrived in Annapolis. Father had been here a year already, and had built us a small, snug house, but he was excited about his plans for a much grander place.

I remembered sitting in front of him on the mare, her rough mane twisted in my fingers and the lovely smells of horse and pine needles and chimney smoke in my nose. We climbed through thick woods along a narrow cart track. Sometimes the branches bent right down and brushed our faces. When we came out of the trees and I saw the huge wooden skeleton of a house with men working high up on the beams, Father says I gasped and clapped my hands. He pointed out where there would be five windows above, and four below, and the space for the wide front door. This, Father had said with a sweep of his arm, was our farm. Below us, rows of apple trees marched up the hill. Behind the house, he told me, there would be a barn, and gardens. As a four-year-old girl I had trouble imagining what he described. Now, looking around me, I smiled to think that I was helping his dream grow.

Even if Father didn't have time for farming, I thought, I will keep the Evans estate prospering. I could envision a whole flock of sheep spread across the pasture, the sound of bells on a team of oxen plowing the field for planting flax and barley, the eggs and butter and wool I could trade for whatever I wanted from anywhere in the world.

I was putting the last rails of the fence in place on the afternoon the hired man arrived. Father had taken Hazel and the cart down to the town wharf to meet him and when I saw them coming up the lane I put away my tools and went into the kitchen to wash my hands.

"They're going around to the front," Sadie said, pointing out the window.

I heard Mother's voice in the hall. "Elizabeth, come out here with me."

I re-knotted my hair and put on my cap and went to stand beside her as Mr. Jefferson stepped through the double doors. The May sun, shining through the fanlight, cast its lovely pattern on the floor and I noticed that he paused for a moment and looked around the spacious hall, at the stairs, the mirror, the standing clock. Then he took off his hat.

"Mr. Jefferson, I wish to introduce you to my wife, Mrs. Evans," Father said. Then, taking my hand and patting it with his typical affectionate gesture, he said, "And this is my daughter, Elizabeth."

"I am happy to meet you," Mr. Jefferson said, and bowed slightly in Mother's direction. His eyes met mine for a brief moment, then I looked down at my shoes.

"Mr. Jefferson," Mother said in her breezy company voice. "We're delighted that you've arrived safely. I do hope your journey was pleasant. Please, come in and make yourself at home." I hadn't expected her to make this kind of fuss over a hired hand. Her attitude would change quickly, I guessed, once the novelty of his presence had faded.

At supper, Father dominated the conversation. I didn't mind, since it gave me an opportunity to observe Mr. Jefferson without calling attention to my curiosity, which Mother would have claimed was extremely unladylike but I considered to be highly practical. He was a man of medium height, rather thin, with a long, oval face. His nose was pointed. His eyes were an unusually light brown.

"You have much in common with those of us who arrived here from New England in the sixties," Father was saying, obviously pleased to have another man in the house. "You're not running away, escaping some form of persecution. You've come hoping to improve your circumstances, searching for prosperity. A bold move, young man; I admire that. I'm sure we'll get along fine, you and I. As for the women"—here he paused and raised his glass in Mother's direction—"as long as you mind your manners and follow orders in the kitchen, you'll be safe enough."

I noticed Mother rolling her eyes. I glared at Father, but he continued, unimpeded.

"Mr. Lovett, our near neighbour across the brook, is one of the township's representatives in the provincial assembly. Of course, in New England we kept all our decision-making at the level of the town meeting, but here we have had to adapt to the different structure of the Nova Scotia government. To my mind, it works well. Though there are many who still complain that we have been robbed of our autonomy, I'm willing to give this new system a fair chance." He put another bite of meat in his mouth and stopped talking long enough to chew.

Mother took advantage of the pause. "Tell us, Mr. Jefferson, how was your voyage? Did you have to travel far from home to reach the ship? Were the seas very rough? Were your fellow passengers decent?"

Mr. Jefferson swallowed carefully. "Sailed from Scarborough. Good company, settlers mostly. No trouble."

Mother's face revealed that she was baffled by his thick Yorkshire accent and deeply disappointed by his lack of conversation skills, but she forced a smile and carried on. "Well, I hope you won't find yourself too lonely here. Perhaps you'll have a chance to acquaint yourself with some of our neighbours soon. The Bencrofts—"

"Ah, Eliza, he'll have too much work to do for gallivanting about the township socializing. Now, as for the crops, last year we harvested fifty bushels of barley and…." Father went on to describe the operation of the farm in great detail. Mother set her wine glass down heavily and pressed her lips together, but said nothing more. She hated farm talk, especially at the table.

Mr. Jefferson cut his meat in small pieces and ate everything on his plate, including a second helping.

I was in no hurry to share my opinions, but Father turned the conversation to me. "Elizabeth can tell you all about our cows," he said. "They're few in number, but mighty in milk. Isn't that right, my dear?"

I hesitated for a moment, unprepared and reluctant to share anything of my cows, but then remembered Daisy's infected teat. After a brief description of her symptoms I explained my treatment method. "It was quite red and swollen and she was obviously in pain," I explained. "I put a poultice on it this morning and again this evening. Tomorrow I will see if it's had any effect." I heard Mother clearing her throat. I'd said too much, as usual.

"Elizabeth has a special gift for working with animals," Father boasted. "And she's as able as any son when it comes to field work."

I knew I was blushing, so I kept my head down and concentrated on my supper.

After Father and Mr. Jefferson had gone out to tour the barn I stared out the window, resisting the urge to run out and join them. There was still work to be done in the kitchen and Father didn't need my help explaining where the harness and the pitchfork were kept. Besides, I didn't want to give the impression that I was eager to be in Mr. Jefferson's company.

"What do you think of him, Sadie?"

"He's here to do a job and it doesn't matter much how I feel, now does it?"

"He'll never be part of the family the way you are." I tried to give her a hug, but she shooed me off.

I lay awake long into the night, listening to the gusty wind and thinking about the new order of our household. I certainly wasn't about to let Mr. Jefferson outdo me in work or in authority. The farm was going to be mine someday—he would need to know that as soon as possible. But he is Father's employee, I thought, and he'll be in charge of the farm when Father's away. Can he tell me what to do? Can I tell him? I threw back my quilts and pulled them up again a dozen times before I could finally sleep.

Chapter Five

It didn't take long for the hired man to reveal his
ambitions. It was planting season, and though we had already
sown the oats, Father was worried about getting the corn
and barley and flax in. The two men spent a day walking the
fields and then sat discussing the work over supper. I heard
Mr. Jefferson say he was sure that he could raise one hundred
bushels of barley where we had raised fifty.

That evening, as I sat at the writing desk in my bedroom
struggling over a letter I was obliged to write to my Boston
cousins, I glanced out the west window and saw the small
figures of Father and Mr. Jefferson walking down the hill
together between the bowing apple trees. I pulled aside the
curtains to watch them. Father was obviously listening, his
hands clasped behind his back, his head tilted to one side. Mr.
Jefferson, I noticed, kept his hands shoved into his pockets,
but once in a while one hand would escape and point, or

gesture, or scratch his ear. They stopped in the middle of the orchard and I saw Father throw back his head and laugh.

I quickly sat at my desk again and tried to continue the letter, but sudden tears obscured the words I had written. What a silly girl you are, I scolded myself, thinking of what Father might say if he saw me.

Mr. Jefferson's presence infuriated me. It wasn't that he did or said anything rude or distasteful, in fact he hardly spoke at all. I couldn't find anything to complain about, not his work habits, his cleanliness, his treatment of the animals. But everywhere I went, he was there first. In the barn, in the orchard, in the kitchen, even in Father's study. All of my favourite places had been taken over by this stranger who knew nothing about our family.

As Father had predicted, there was little time for socializing, but Mr. Jefferson had his initiation into the community the day they went down to Sawmill Creek to net alewife. When they didn't return by late afternoon, Sadie sent me down with a basket of supper.

The water was full of the dark shapes of frenzied fish. Each scoop of a net brought up a hundred silvery, flopping bodies that were dumped into baskets to slowly suffocate. I knew well that working the net while balanced on the wet rocks wasn't easy, and was delighted to see that Mr.

Jefferson was not skilled at the task. Just as he raised his pole to dip the net in the water, he lost his balance and fell over backward with a tremendous splash. One of the Bencroft brothers retrieved him, and the net, and brought them over to the bank where I stood, laughing along with everyone else.

Father threw a blanket over his shoulders and patted him vigorously on the back. "Don't worry, Jefferson, you'll get the hang of it."

"I brought your supper," I said, nudging the basket with the toe of my shoe. I reached out for the net, to give him a demonstration of proper technique, but Father picked it up first.

"He'll give it another try in a minute, Elizabeth." He nodded toward a basket full of the fish he had already caught. "You can take that load up to the house when you go."

I turned away to head for home, flapping at the little blackflies that were trying to climb into my ears and under my cap. If having this hired man meant I would have to spend my time stuck between the rows of the garden or in the kitchen, I was sure it was a bad arrangement. The only reason I had for accepting his presence was to stop Father from selling the farm. I shifted the weight of the smelly load to my other hip and prepared myself to be miserable.

Over the next few days Sadie and I worked together turning over the soil in the vegetable garden. My hands ached by the end of every afternoon. One morning, when Mother was feeling strong, even she came out to help. She did a little digging and raking, but most of her energy went into talking. When I worked beside her in one row she was silent for a long time. I was about to ask if she needed a rest when she spoke.

"I'm thinking of making a trip to Massachusetts this spring."

"I thought New England was in too much turmoil for you to even consider a visit. Father's newspapers from Boston say there's sure to be a blockade of the harbour."

"Oh, that's ridiculous. It's all just for show. There's no real threat. Besides, I've put it off far too long," she said firmly. "Mrs. Wolseley's travelling on the next schooner, so I would have company."

"Does Father know?"

"We have discussed it," she said, her face set in an expression that I knew meant that they'd had an argument, and that Mother had won, as usual. Then she grasped my hand. "Elizabeth, I want you to come with me. I know your Uncle William would be happy to have you stay with them and you could finally meet all your cousins. Please say you will. Just for a visit."

If she had asked me only a few months earlier I would have rejected the idea immediately. Instead, I heard myself saying, "I'll think about it."

She looked as surprised as I felt. She had expected me to say no, as I had done every other time the subject had been raised by her or anyone else. She let go of my hand and, just before going inside, said with a rare genuine smile, "I would enjoy your company."

After supper, I went for a walk out on the marsh. The flat fields and the open sky above my head seemed to make it a good place for hard decisions. Rays of sunlight struggling through the clouds fell on the hills, lighting up patches of new green leaves.

The good thing about going to Sudbury with Mother, I reasoned, is being free of the annoying Mr. Jefferson. But who would take care of the cows? I looked down at my calloused, brown hands. Would I feel any more comfortable, or free in my uncle's house? Would my cousins welcome me? Maybe among them I would find some real friendship. And maybe, I thought with a tingle of excitement, I could visit Boston.

The clouds obscured the sun again. I reminded myself that Mother would undoubtedly parade me past an endless list of eligible young men who would have no appreciation for my farming skills. And I would miss the strawberries, and the taste of fresh trout, and the startling cold of the brook water on hot skin. I wouldn't be able to ride the full hay cart across the marsh in the evening light or listen to Sadie humming while she kneaded bread. And I would miss Father.

It was close to dark before I turned for home, still undecided. As I came up the lane toward the house I could see the silhouettes of Father and Mr. Jefferson in the kitchen. I felt more forlorn than ever. Father has no need for my help anymore, I thought, and no time for my company.

When I came inside, he was alone in front of the kitchen fire.

"I have been trying to make a decision," I said. I stayed by the door.

"I know. Your mother told me and I have been dwelling on it all evening."

"What do you think?"

"Your mother's arguments are valid. It would be enriching for you to see her family again. I'm sure you don't remember them. They are good people, and well positioned in Sudbury society. Your grandfather was a judge, you know. And your uncle a deacon."

"I know all that." The fire spat an ember onto the hearth. I sat down beside him.

"There is one thing that prevents me from wholeheartedly endorsing your trip."

I waited, clutching my skirt in both fists.

"I am afraid, if you went to Sudbury, you would discover the pleasures of life there, and you would find some handsome lieutenant and become engaged and never return. And though it may be selfish of me to say so, I think that would break my heart."

I laughed right out loud at his words and threw my arms around his neck. "Oh, Father, now I know what my answer will be!" I ran through the hall and into the kitchen, hollering to Sadie as I passed her, "I'm staying, I'm staying!" I kept on going, out the door and around the corner of the house and right into Mr. Jefferson as he came from the other direction. The next thing I knew, I was sitting in the grass, still laughing.

He helped me to my feet. "Are you hurt?"

"No," I was still laughing, and he was still holding my arm. "I'm just happy. I've decided not to go away."

"You should be more careful." He let go and went into the house.

At bedtime, I started for the sitting room to say goodnight to Mother. I stopped when I heard voices raised in argument. I strained to make out the words being spoken behind the partly open door. The lamplight fell into an angled shape on the hall floor near my feet.

"She had virtually decided to go with me, Henry," my mother was saying, with more force than I had heard from her in months. "But you persuaded her to stay here, with you. How could you be so selfish?"

"Calm yourself, my dear," Father began in his slow and reasonable voice. "I merely told her the truth about my feelings, just as she asked me to. She was thinking of going with you only because she was feeling angry and resentful. Even you could see that. She did not want to go for the right reasons."

"Perhaps not, but once there she would have had so many of the right opportunities. She is at the age when she should have introductions, proper influences. Instead, you keep her here, treating her like the son you wished for and not the daughter she is. Farming, indeed. What kind of life is that for a young lady?"

"It is her life, Eliza."

Mother was silent. Probably mustering a new argument, I thought. I admired her at that moment for her ability to stand up to him when she really needed to, when it was a matter of principle. Father's forceful style and clear logic always wore me down too quickly and our disputes usually ended with me in tears and Father in the role of comforter. But Mother seemed to have her emotions surprisingly well in hand. She forged ahead, intent on her need to convince him.

"You promised, all those years ago when we first planned to come here, that you would ensure Elizabeth's proper education. I do not believe you have lived up to that promise." Those words, I knew, would strike at Father's core.

"I have done my best." I heard him sigh. Then his voice seemed to regain some strength. "She has skills that will serve her well in this community."

"But what of other communities? What of the wider world, of Halifax, of Boston, for heaven's sake?" There was a pause, and I made myself ready to dash away quickly should one of them emerge, but Mother continued. "I had been hoping that if Elizabeth came to Sudbury with me this spring—"

I could stay outside the room no longer. I pushed open the door and stepped into the full lamplight. "I believe I should have a say in what I do with my life." I looked from my mother's face to my father's, refusing to feel sorry for having trespassed on their conversation.

"Oh, Elizabeth, this is exactly the kind of behaviour I'm concerned about." Mother was scowling.

"But I should be part of this discussion. You have to hear what I want."

Father put a hand on Mother's arm. "Let the girl have her say, for heaven's sake. She deserves that much."

"As long as you act in a civilized manner," Mother relented.

"I would like to go to Sudbury someday, but not now. I would only get into trouble. I would embarrass you terribly. Everyone would gossip about how unladylike I am, and I would make everyone uncomfortable, especially you, Mother. Your reputation would suffer."

"My reputation is secure, but I do not wish for you to be looked upon as an ill-mannered, ignorant daughter."

"Eliza!" Father interrupted her this time. "The girl is hardly ignorant. She reads more than I ever did at her age, she knows the care of cows and the spinning of wool and every plant in the garden. She makes the best butter in the township, and you said yourself just the other day that her pies are improving."

So, I thought, Mother had actually complimented me. She looked flustered to have had this revealed and continued talking to Father as if I wasn't in the room.

"My point is simply that if I go and leave Elizabeth here, the two of you will only pay attention to what is important to you, and I will come back to find a monster where there should be a young lady."

"Monster! Mother, I am not about to change form altogether just because I like to get my hands dirty and my feet wet." I paused for a breath then took a new direction in my persuasion. "Besides, I am needed here. I work hard and if I leave, all my work will have to be done by someone else. Father has already said he has too many commitments and Mr. Jefferson certainly cannot be expected to look after my chores. Who would do my share of the spinning, churning, washing, and mending? I won't have Sadie taking on my responsibilities. She works too hard as it is." Just then a dreadful thought occurred to me. "Unless you plan to take Sadie with you."

"I had not yet decided," Mother said. "But I would certainly not dare to take her and leave you here."

"Let me suggest something, Eliza," Father intervened. "What if Elizabeth and I promise that she will make an effort to find some appropriate friends in town this summer, attend whatever social occasions she can, and that she will make at least one trip with me to Halifax where we will buy her some dresses?"

"I don't need any dresses!" I blurted out. Father hushed me.

Mother folded her arms. "Do you both promise you will abide by this? And Henry you will help her and if you are not here you will be sure Sadie reminds her of her promise?"

"Yes," Father said with a solemn face. They looked at me, their naughty child.

"Yes," I said. Once I had decided to stay I was determined that I would make whatever concessions were necessary.

"And," Mother held up an imposing index finger, "if I return to find that you two have been neglecting your promise to me, I will turn right around and take you with me, Elizabeth. No arguments. Do I make myself clear?"

Father and I both nodded and we all went off to bed.

Chapter Six

❧

By the time May came to a close Sadie and I had finished planting the turnips, cabbage, carrots, onions, and watermelon in the kitchen garden, and Mr. Jefferson had the other crops in the ground. When he came inside for meals I noticed that his face and neck and arms were already brown and freckled from the sun, although he always rolled down his shirt sleeves before he sat at the table for meals.

"You could have asked me to help with the plowing," I said to Father one morning after Mr. Jefferson had already left the house. Father was reading while the remains of his breakfast got cold on the table. I was skimming cream from the top of the milk that had been collecting in the cellar all week. The sour smell filled the kitchen. I poured the cream into the churn and began to slowly raise and lower the dasher, careful to keep the motion steady and slow. "There was no need for Mr. Jefferson to do it all."

"That is what I hired him for, my dear," Father said, looking over the top of the newspaper. "And now that the planting's done, he'll start on clearing some land for next year. I couldn't have hired any better man."

"Surely we have no need for more fields—we're not even using all the marshland we own." I could feel the tempo of my churning getting faster with my agitation.

"Well, as I've said before, the dykes won't last forever and the sea will reclaim the land that was never meant to be farmed in the first place. Mr. Jefferson is very much in favour of turning more to upland farming, and I am willing to follow his advice on this." He folded his paper and got up from the table.

"You'll be ruining the butter if you keep that up," Sadie grumbled. "Let me do it." I gladly gave over the job. I escaped the heat of the morning kitchen and ran down across the field to Lovett's Brook and my solitude. As I lay in the wild mint and forget-me-not, watching the water skippers dance across the surface of the pool, I thought about what Father had said. I had begun to feel a grudging admiration for Mr. Jefferson's work habits, but I was not willing to hand the farm to him to do with as he pleased. The hay and barley had been growing splendidly on the marshlands for years—there was no need to push farther up the hill and waste time and effort clearing forested land.

The soil wasn't nearly as rich. Mr. Jefferson was acting as if he owned the place. I trailed my fingers in the numbing water.

When I returned to the house Sadie reminded me that the turnip patch needed attention. I took the hoe and climbed over the fence. Weeding was a tiring and shadeless job that always seemed to need doing again as soon as it was finished. The lamb's quarter and pigweed would take over the whole garden if given the chance, and the turnips weren't strong enough yet to defend themselves. I usually tried to make sure I'd finished the task before the sun was high, but my visit to the brook had its consequences. Perspiration trickled down the back of my neck.

I had settled nicely into the rhythm of the job when a movement near the fence caught my attention. I raised the brim of my hat just enough, without stopping the motion of the hoe, to see Mr. Jefferson leaning against the fence. Probably deciding that this would be a better spot for cabbages, I thought.

"You need my sisters," he said abruptly, and I realized it was the first time I'd heard him begin a conversation.

"Pardon me?" I stopped and stood straight.

"I have five sisters," he said. "Good weeders."

"How convenient." I began hoeing again, the dirt spraying

up as I struck at each offensive plant. I thought he might move off, but he stayed where he was.

"Three brothers. Would have been four but one died."

"I'm sorry."

"He was run down by a horse and wagon in the village." He didn't sound sorrowful to me, just calm and matter-of-fact. "Youngest is eight. Mother says he won't sleep in the house since I've gone. Stays in the barn with the horses."

I had worked my way closer to the fence as he talked and when he stopped I was only a row away. I paused to wipe my forehead with my apron.

"Do you ever wish you had brothers and sisters?" he asked. "So you didn't have to do all this work alone?"

"I'm quite happy working alone," I said. I knew I sounded rude, but I just wanted him to leave me be and to quit bragging about his huge family. "Besides, I like my family exactly the way it has been since I was born." I went on chopping at the weeds. I could hear a cow bellowing from the pasture.

"I'd best get back to work," he said, and was gone as suddenly as he had appeared. Apparently, my strategy had worked.

A few days later Father and I made a trip into town together. He had business at the courthouse, and I was bound for the store. We sat side by side on the seat, Father holding the reins loosely and letting Hazel make her own easy way down the narrow and bumpy cart track that ran all the way to the mill. We talked about little things—Father's latest trip to Halifax, the names of the birds that twittered at us as we passed, books we had read.

When we came over the last rise and around the long slow corner before town, we could see the chimneys of the fort and beyond them the river where it widened into the basin. Soon we were clattering along the cobbled street of the town. My eyes took in the shabbiness of broken shingles on some of the buildings, the dullness of many of their windows. Several houses along our route were boarded up and empty.

I knew the town had not always been so quiet and shabby. It was Halifax, Father had said, that had changed Annapolis Royal for the worse. When the government moved the garrison to the new capital many of the inhabitants and much of the business followed, leaving poor Annapolis bereft. I was glad the soldiers were gone. The town would have been noisy and crowded, full of people trying to impress each other. Instead, it was unfashionable and peaceful.

Inside the store, Mr. Wolseley was behind the counter, as always, and he greeted me with a warm smile and a flurry of news as I let my eyes browse the shelves behind him.

"I finally got that shipment of tobacco your Father's been waiting for, Miss Evans," he said. "And what do you hear from Massachusetts? Those Yankees are stirring up trouble for themselves, and us too, likely. I hope your mother's family's got a good stockpile of tea since there's none getting past Boston Harbour from what I've heard. "

"I imagine they have what they need," I replied with a laugh. Then I lifted my heavy baskets up to the counter and began to unload my goods. Mr. Wolseley accepted each item, unwrapped it, and took a close look. While I waited, I breathed in the exotic scents of molasses, tea, and spices.

"As always, Miss Evans, you bring me lovely goods," he said as he unwrapped the large piece of fine, pale butter I'd brought. He ran his hand across the bolt of linen and smelled the cheese, then opened his account book and began jotting figures. My goods were still listed under Father's name, but I looked forward to the time when I would have my own account, under my own name. "And what is it that you'll be needing today?" he asked when he was finished.

I pulled my list from my pocket and smoothed it on the counter. As I read out the items, Mr. Wolseley plunked each one in front of me with a storekeeper's satisfaction. Molasses, four hinges, salt, two shoe heels, thread, tobacco, paper, and cloves. He noted each item in his book.

"That will be everything, I think, Mr. Wolseley."

"Perhaps I should show you this broadcloth that came not long ago in a shipment from England. Makes lovely skirts and aprons."

"I don't need any today, but you've reminded me of the ticking I was supposed to buy. Mr. Jefferson's bed is just about falling apart and Mother is embarrassed that we haven't fixed it up yet."

"How is he working out? He's been at your place a few months, eh?"

"Since planting time. He's a hard worker."

"So I've heard. Your father says he may be doing some clearing this year."

"Yes, Mr. Jefferson believes that cleared upland is better than the marshland for crops." I tried to keep my tone neutral.

"Oh, I see. Well, those Yorkshiremen aren't too familiar with the dykelands, you know. He'll probably see the good of them come September when he's harvesting marsh hay."

I had nothing more to say on the subject. Mr. Wolseley finished writing up my account and wrapping my purchases and we said our goodbyes.

Outside the store I stood in the street for a moment, wondering what to do with myself until Father was free. I heard my name called and turned to see Charlotte scampering towards me. She held her skirts up to avoid the mud. "Elizabeth, I'm so glad I caught you. I want to invite you on a picnic."

"A picnic." I wasn't sure what else to say. I thought of my promise to Mother about social occasions and wondered if this would count.

"I do hope you can join us," Charlotte was chattering on. "Susannah and Amelia, my friends from town, are coming too. Amelia is nearly sixteen, so she's closer to your age and they're both wanting to be more acquainted with you. Please say you'll accept."

I found her exuberance amusing. "Well, first you should tell me when you're going on this picnic."

"Next Tuesday. We are going to meet at the ferry and go across to Granville for the day. Susannah says she knows of a lovely spot on the river where her cousins live. Jonas Farnsworth is one of her cousins. Perhaps he'll come along. I've heard he's considered quite a catch." She waved across the street to several passing ladies.

"I don't care about Jonas Farnsworth one bit," I told her, "but I would like to go on the picnic. What shall I bring?"

"If you would bring some bread and butter—we all know what delicious butter you make—that would be perfect. Susannah is bringing cold meat pies, and I'm bringing a cake.

Too bad the strawberries won't be ready, but Amelia said she's sure her mother still has some preserves, or maybe even strawberry cordial from last year."

"I'll meet you at the ferry landing after my chores are finished."

"I'm so glad. Till Tuesday, then." Charlotte was off again, tripping back along the street to where her father stood talking to a group of men.

Chapter Seven

On Tuesday morning, as I called the cows in from their night pasture, I knew the summer was beginning. The sky was full of pale pink streaks, and though the sun was still hidden by the mountain, the air had a warm softness that comes only in June.

The barn was cool and quiet. My movements sent the dust motes sailing. I left the doors open wide to let in the sweet dewy air and to hear the best of the early birds—the bobolink who came to the corner fence post, the white-throated sparrow whose voice carried down from the edge of the woods. I was strongly tempted to abandon my social obligation and stay at home. Charlotte wouldn't be too hurt, I thought. Hazel nickered.

"Don't fret," I told her, running my fingers through her tangled forelock. "Breakfast is coming."

I climbed the ladder to the mow where there was still a

small pile of last year's hay. Using the pitchfork, I began tossing smaller mounds of it down to the lower floor. I was about to climb back down when Mr. Jefferson came into the barn. He didn't notice me, but went about the barn obviously searching for something. He poked his head over the door into Hazel's stall, then checked the various hooks and nails sticking out of the beams, most of them burdened with harnesses, horseshoes, scythes, and other implements.

"Are you looking for something?"

He looked up then and saw me standing above him. "Piece of rope."

"Did my father say it was in the barn?"

"Yes."

"What does he need it for?"

"Not sure." He went on searching, checking behind the bins where the oats were stored.

"Father told me you plan to do some clearing this year."

"Some."

"Have you chosen an area yet?"

"It's up to the Colonel."

"He also said you were looking for a farm lot for yourself. Where, Cornwallis, Horton?" I tried my best to sound casual, but knew I wasn't convincing.

"You don't know where the extra rope is." It wasn't a question.

"No." I tossed down one more forkful of hay, barely missing him.

Mr. Jefferson turned and strode through the barn doors and across the yard. I stepped down the ladder and went to work milking the cows.

As I held the pasture gate open to let them back out to graze, I realized that some new faces and new conversations might be a good thing after all. I left my apron in the kitchen and put the promised bread and butter in a basket. Sadie gave me some of her pickles.

"Make sure you wear your shoes, Elizabeth," said Mother. "And keep the sun off your face."

"All right," I grumbled. I took the wide-brimmed hat from the peg on the wall. At the bottom of the orchard I paused long enough to tuck my shoes in a hollow tree. Then I took the path out toward the river. Mother would have insisted on the main road, but I knew I could make better time and have a more interesting walk if I went along the dykes.

The wind met me as I came out of the trees. It sang through the long grasses in the marsh and they danced and made an ocean of green, rippling waves. The smell of clover was strong here, mixed with cows, and mud, and whatever scents the wind had brought in from the basin—a little salty, a little summery.

Charlotte and her companions Amelia and Susannah were waiting for me at the ferry landing when I arrived. They didn't look as windblown as I'm sure I must have, and they were wearing much fancier outfits. They all greeted me warmly and we loaded our baskets and ourselves into Mr. Clarke's boat for the trip across the river.

Susannah shut her eyes tight as the ferry lurched a little when Mr. Clarke settled into his place. "Oh, I don't like this," she groaned. "How long will it take to cross?"

"What's the trouble, miss? Afraid of the water, are ye?"

"Yes, I am. Terribly afraid. And of fish, too."

We all laughed and Mr. Clarke pulled hard on his oars. "I'll get ye across in no time."

My back was warm with the morning sun and my face cool from the west wind by the time we'd crossed the river, its water reflecting blue of sky over red-brown mud. Mr. Clarke handed each of us carefully onto the wharf and we paid him our fare.

"We'll be returning at three o'clock, Mr. Clarke. Will you take us over again?" Charlotte was the leader of our expedition and took her role seriously.

"Oh, well, I suppose ye could convince me, 'specially if ye save a piece of that cake for me." He winked at Charlotte, who blushed from her hairline to her collar.

A man carrying a young pig was making his way down the track to the wharf as we climbed up from the river.

"I'm relieved to not be riding across with him," Susannah said, shuddering.

"She's afraid of pigs too," Amelia said. "What a baby you are, Su."

I ran ahead a short way to be the first to see the view from the high bank. I could look right out to the mouth of the river and into the basin from this spot. There was the fort, its three sturdy chimneys and the spire of the church showing over the rampart, and there the shops and houses of the town, the wharves and masts of the harbour, and beyond them all, the sparkling waters of the open basin. The green hills sloped down to the water and the marshes stretched back on either side of the river behind me.

By the time they all caught up to me again, Susannah was telling about visiting her Granville cousins. "Once, Mama and I were stuck there for two weeks when there was a bad storm. The snow was right up to the second-storey windows on the north side of the house. The boys were perfectly dreadful to me, and they expected me to do all the cooking!"

I watched for violets along the edges of the path and smelled the cool air from the river.

"Isn't this lovely!" Charlotte exclaimed as we arrived at the chosen spot. A grove of birch trees offered lacy shade and dazzling white lines against the dark woods. An oak tree spread its branches to form an open, grassy spot. Charlotte laid out her blanket.

"Let's eat something now, I'm starving." Amelia pulled her skirts around her and settled on one corner. I offered up my bread and butter and Sadie's pickles, Susannah brought out her meat pies, and Amelia began pouring the strawberry cordial. It was too sweet for my taste, but a beautiful colour.

After we'd eaten our fill, we all leaned back on our elbows. Someone let out a satisfied groan. I thought I might fall asleep in the warm sun.

Charlotte broke the stillness. "Susannah, didn't you say your cousin Jonas might come?"

"Sounds like Charlotte fancies him," Amelia said.

"Don't be silly. I haven't even met him yet."

Amelia tried a new target. "I hear there's a new man at your place, Elizabeth."

I was surprised the news had travelled already.

"Have you met him, Charlotte? What's he like?" Amelia's voice was loud and harsh.

Charlotte glanced at me. "I've only seen him from a distance, planting or whatever, but I would say he is rather good-looking."

"Well, when will you set the wedding date?" Amelia rubbed her hands together.

I didn't know if she was talking to me or to Charlotte, but I wasn't interested in listening. I stood up and stretched. "I feel like exploring. What's down over that slope, Susannah?"

"Oh, come along, I'll show you." She jumped up eagerly. Charlotte and Amelia stayed where they were. As soon as we were out of earshot, Susannah said, "Don't listen to Amelia. She's mean to everyone."

She led me to a collection of stones, all fairly large, arranged in a rectangular pattern. Not far away was another, smaller grouping.

"My cousins always say that there are ghosts here," Susannah said. Her voice was so hushed I realized she believed them.

"Well, they're not going to bother us on a bright day like today." I began to step along the line of rocks, balancing carefully on their smooth, rounded forms. "Whose house was on this foundation? Do you know? It hasn't had a structure on it for many years."

"My uncle says it was a French family that lived here. They had a farm and a woodlot that ran up the side of the mountain." She gestured to the North Mountain's ridge behind us.

"Maybe the family moved to a bigger house and this one just collapsed and disappeared over the years," I suggested, jumping to solid ground. We began to walk back toward the picnic site. I wanted to get a piece of cake before Amelia ate it all.

"Jonas, my cousin, says all the people were murdered by Indians and that on full moon nights they come crying down over the mountain, looking for their animals and their belongings. He says people have seen a woman in a long, white shift wandering around this foundation as if she's lost something." Her eyes were wide and she shivered a little.

"What are you two whispering about?" Amelia called out to us.

"Ghosts," Susannah told her. "And Indians."

"My father says that the Mi'kmaq people have been unfairly treated and should have our sympathy," claimed Charlotte.

"My father always curses them. He says they're dirty and drunk and good for nothing," Amelia said.

I listened to them argue back and forth about Indians, and fathers, and ghosts while I watched the sun on the river and the terns dipping and skimming the waves.

"Jonas!" Susannah cried. She ran toward a tall young man who was stepping out of the trees. Charlotte followed.

I went back to the ruins. Running my hands over the stones, I tried to imagine the lives that had been lived inside their sturdy protection. Then something caught my eye. Something metal, wedged between the stones. As I reached for it, I thought of the ghostly woman from Susannah's story. I had heard many tales of spirits, but for the first time I felt prickles on the back of my neck. Maybe she really did walk these ruins. Was this the object she searched for? It must be precious to have kept her from her rest, I thought. I could barely grasp it to wiggle it free. As I heard Charlotte calling my name the object came loose and fell into my palm. It was a small cross bearing a tiny figure of the crucified Christ. The metal was rough with corrosion, but still sturdy, and still beautiful. Charlotte called my name again. I slipped the cross into my pocket and climbed up over the stones to join the picnickers.

Susannah introduced me to Jonas, who sat on the grass eating a piece of Charlotte's cake. I noticed that he had taken off his cap and his hair lay flattened against his freckled forehead. He nodded in my direction, then began teasing Charlotte by pulling at her hair ribbons and trying to take her shoe. She giggled.

Jonas accompanied our little group back to the ferry wharf, singing along with Susannah's high voice. He let Amelia convince him to tell about the ghosts as we waited for the ferry. I paid close attention, but the story was mostly boasting, as he told it, and offered little insight into my intriguing discovery.

"What foolishness are ye spreading now, young Jonas?" Mr. Clarke's voice rang out across the short span of choppy water as he approached. He hadn't even needed to turn his head to know the owner of the confident voice. "Haven't ye got better things to do than hang about bothering my passengers?"

Jonas looked embarrassed and said his goodbyes quickly, kissing Charlotte's hand before running off up the path toward his farm.

"Don't pay a bit of attention to that one," Mr. Clarke said as he handed us into the boat. "Oh, I know, Miss Susannah, he's your cousin and all, but he's a devil of a troublemaker. Cut my boat loose on more than one occasion, he has. And scared the living wits right out of Mrs. Clarke's head one night. I thought she'd never recover. Had her swooning in her bed for a fortnight!" Mr. Clarke's face had begun to turn red as he pulled vigorously on the oars. He was a rather comical figure, spluttering and fuming as he sat hunched on the seat. I saw Charlotte and Amelia cover their mouths. Their eyes were full of laughter.

"What happened?" I asked.

"Had her convinced she was seeing ghosts, he did, over by the ruins one night in winter. We was going home from playing cards with the Prescotts. Young Jonas had hung a length of cloth from a tree and was making weird sounds. Caught him. Made him tell the truth. I should have hided him while I had him, but Mrs. Clarke was so distraught I had to leave him be. I've never forgiven him. Never."

The stifled giggles subsided as we all recognized his genuine anger and we rode the rest of the way in silence. I let my fingers trace the form of my secret treasure through the cloth of my pocket.

Mother demanded a detailed description of every moment of the outing, including the trimmings on each girl's dress. I couldn't even remember the colour of Charlotte's hair ribbons.

Before I went to bed, I wrapped the cross in a handkerchief and reached into the back of my writing desk to tuck it into a corner. I thought of the ghostly woman until I fell asleep.

On the morning Mother was to board the ship for Boston, she came into my room while I was dressing. Outside the windows gloomy, low clouds hung over the hills. I couldn't decide if my mood had more to do with the weather or with Mother's departure.

"I have something for you, my dear," she said in the doorway, holding her hands behind her back. She was dressed in travelling clothes made of dark, heavy cloth that stood up well to all sorts of weather and cramped quarters. I was still in my shift and petticoat and my hair was loose.

"I know you will turn eighteen while I am away and I want you to have this as a gift." She drew out a small book.

Etiquette rules, I thought with a silent groan. Or instructions for card games.

"It's a diary. I bought it the last time I went to Halifax with your father. It has lovely pages for your writing. Just feel the paper."

I took the book from her hand and held it, surprised and a little bewildered. What did I want with a diary?

She began to braid my hair. "I know you've never been fond of letter-writing, but I thought perhaps you could try to write down the things that you do, people you meet, events you attend, even the subject of the Sunday sermon, if it moves you. There's nothing like a daily record of your activities to help you see how time is passing and to remember important events. Even the weather, and the food you've eaten. Many women keep diaries; it's very fashionable."

"I'm not sure I would have any time."

"A few minutes every morning, or in the evening before

you go to bed. That's all it takes, and later you'll be so glad you did."

"Do you keep a diary?"

"I haven't for years, but I did when I was your age. The winters I lived with my grandparents in Boston, attending school, I kept a diary. Grandmother encouraged me, since it improved my penmanship, and it served as a record of my activities and lessons that I could share with my parents when I returned home."

"Oh." I understood her motive now. This was simply a way for her to spy on me, to know whether or not I was keeping my promise to improve myself, to become more like her.

"Thank you, Mother," I said, forcing a smile as I ran my hand over the dark blue cover. I wondered if she had saved those diaries of hers. What did she write about? Did she miss her parents? Her home? Did she make friends easily at school? Did she read her entries again as an adult and wish she could go back in time? I put the diary on my writing desk, kissed Mother's cheek, and told her I'd be dressed and downstairs in a moment.

The wharf was crowded with people standing in the heavy mist. We found Mrs. Wolseley and her young son, who looked pale and frightened as he stood shivering and holding his mother's hand. When I tried to show him the men climbing the rigging of the ship he hid his face against her leg.

Mother shed more than a few tears and clutched her soggy handkerchief close to her face as she accepted our kisses on her cheek. Just as she was about to step across to the schooner, she turned and gripped my hand with a strength that surprised me. I thought she was going to speak, but a man bumped me from behind and I stumbled. When I regained my balance, Mother had turned away and was being helped down onto the deck.

Father and I waved, the men untied the thick lines, the sails rose in the grey morning air, and the ship departed. We watched as it moved slowly across the quiet waters of the basin, heading for the gap in the black ridge of the North Mountain. I thought of the rough weather the small ship might encounter once she reached the open water of the bay. For a moment I almost wished I were aboard.

Chapter Eight

❧

*A*fter Mother's departure, the summer turned hot and aside from a few short showers early in July, we had no rain. On my birthday, Sadie made a cake, but the weather was so uncomfortably humid that the whole household was in a sullen mood.

I didn't bother to record these facts in my diary, nor did I record that I caught twenty-two trout in Lovett's Brook before the water level dropped too low for the fish, nor that Charlotte went off with her father to Cumberland for a month, nor that Sadie's feet had swelled up with the heat and she grew more cranky with each passing day. I was conscious of the empty book in the desk, but each time I tried to write something, my doubts overcame me. Mother wouldn't want to read about cows and crops, I thought, and she wouldn't want to read about brook trout and watermelons. I shoved the diary farther into the corner, out of sight.

I did write several short letters to Mother, reporting on the poor sermons of the visiting minister and the unusual weather. She, in turn, wrote news of her family—all the births, weddings, illnesses, and deaths that had taken place since her last visit. I could tell from her words she was happy to be home again.

One afternoon in August, after a cold lunch of bread and cucumber slices and blueberry pie, Father went off to pack his bag. He was due in court the next morning. Sadie disappeared into her room for a rest and I escaped to the shade of the orchard with Mother's latest letter.

I had dozed off when I heard Sadie's voice drifting down from the house. I couldn't make out the words, but the tone told me that she was more agitated than usual. In another moment Mr. Jefferson was coming towards me. He wiped his forehead with his sleeve as he peered under the overhanging branches.

"Sadie's looking for you," he said.

I groaned. "Now what? Can't that woman just let things be for a few hours when it's this hot?"

"Apparently not. She said something about washing quilts. Asked if I'd seen you. Perhaps you should give her a hand."

"If you think I'm going to do whatever you tell me—" I stopped myself before I said anything more. He was only trying to help Sadie, I thought. "I'll go and see," I muttered, half wishing I'd let myself finish the sentence, just to blow off some steam.

Sadie was indeed getting ready to do washing and had the tub out on the grass.

"At least put it in the shade, for heaven's sake," I snapped in exasperation. "That way when you die of the heat we won't have to move your body right away."

She pushed up her sleeves and plunged the washboard and soap into the water. "Are you just going to stand there?"

"We don't have to do this now, Sadie."

"No better time. Now, bring those quilts over." She gestured to the basket by the kitchen door.

And so we scrubbed and rinsed and hung out quilts that didn't really need washing, until I thought I would faint. When I finally persuaded Sadie to pause for a drink of water she looked exhausted. I brought the milking stool out for her, and sat on the ground beside it.

"Mr. Jefferson found your hiding place, did he?"

"I was only trying to stay cool and read Mother's letter."

"Hmph. I hope he soon gets around to asking you to marry him. I'm getting tired of waiting."

"If you're trying to make me angry, it won't work. I'm too hot."

"I know he's thinking about it. He's got that look to him."

"What are you talking about? He's no different than ever. All he thinks about is working and eating."

"Oh, is that so? Then why'd he go and buy a new shirt at Wolseley's last week? And two collars?"

That surprised me. What would Mr. Jefferson want with store-bought shirts? "Probably for church," I said. "Or maybe he's planning on courting someone."

"Like who?"

I didn't respond.

"I tell you, Betsy, the only person he has his eye on is you. He's just waiting for the right time."

That was too much. I stood and glared down at her. "Sadie, I've heard enough. Don't ever talk to me about Mr. Jefferson, or marriage, or even new shirts. Now let's finish this washing so I can be free of you."

We washed and rinsed the last quilt in a flurry of splashing water. When they were all hanging limply on the line I told her I was going for a walk and that she shouldn't wait for me for supper. She said nothing, and went in the house.

I still felt so angry that I didn't even pay attention to the path my feet took and by the time I had calmed enough to recognize where I was going, I was heading up the hill, towards the woods. The air seemed to press against me,

humid and close, as I climbed the path along the edge of
the cornfield. When I turned to see the view I noticed the
thunderclouds, typical for a hot afternoon, rising over the
mountain. Their boiling shapes were a perfect match for my
tumultuous feelings.

When the field ended the forest closed in with its lovely
sphagnum and damp earth smells. I heard the voice of one
warbler, then only my feet on the path and the soft brushing
of my skirt against the bowing ferns. When I reached the
brook, I crouched and cupped my hand to drink. In spring
the water would rage down the hillside with the strength of
a draft horse in full gallop, but in this dry summer it was a
feeble trickle. As I wiped my mouth I heard the first rumble
of thunder in the far distance.

After a short rest I began to follow the brook's path,
splashing in the water where it collected, gripping the mossy
rocks with my toes. All my resentment was washed from
me and I felt only the clear joy of being alone in the forest.
I thought about other times of the year when I came to
this spot. I loved it in winter, when the water's motion was
captured under the frozen, sculpted surface and the gurgling
turned to thrumming in the hollow, frozen caves. And in
spring, when I sought the mayflowers and lady's slippers and
slapped at the bugs.

Noticing a patch of colourful lichen growing in a rocky outcrop above the stream bed, I left the cool water and climbed the steep bank. At the top, I found a faint path and followed it in idle curiosity. After a short distance I decided it must be a deer path, judging by the droppings I noticed here and there. A stand of birch caught my eye, gleaming white in the dim light of the cloudy afternoon. I continued on, bewitched by this unfamiliar part of the forest, ignoring the repetitious rolling of the thunder in the valley and paying little heed to the increasing patter of rain. One minute only a few drops were falling from the leaves and the next minute a torrent rushed through the branches, making watery curtains. A flash of lightning brightened the gloomy sky and the thunder came again, almost immediately.

I felt my heart beating harder and my breath coming in shorter bursts, but I tried to keep myself calm as I turned to retrace my steps. Thunderstorms did not frighten me. Was it this way, I thought, or that? The crack of the thunder was just above the treetops. I covered my ears. It sounded like the sky was splitting open. I picked my way carefully around the pile of rocks where I thought I had found the lichen, expecting to see the brook close by. It was not there.

I finally admitted to myself that I was scared. My hands trembled. I wasn't used to feeling overwhelmed this way.

I tried to listen for the gurgle of running water, but it was useless. All I heard was the rush of rain and the crack of thunder on top of lightning, and then the wind as it came up over the top of the mountain and down upon me. I could barely see beyond my own arm's length. My clothes were heavy. My sleeves and skirt caught on the branches, pulling me one way, then the other.

When I tripped on a root I fell hard, hitting my knee on a rock. I put my face in my muddy, shaking hands. I told Sadie not to wait on me for supper, but she was going to make meat pie, my favourite, with new potatoes and carrots and turnip. The safety of home seemed so far away that my fear turned suddenly to despair. Oh, I thought, what will happen to me? If I die, Mother and Father will have no one. Father will sell the farm and go to live in Halifax. Perhaps he'll sell Sadie too, and she'll be sent away to live with a cruel master. My thoughts were blowing in circles, making me dizzy. I wanted to lie down right there and go to sleep. I was so tired.

Enough of this silliness, I heard a voice inside me saying, you must find some place to get out of the wind. I used a tree trunk to drag myself to my feet. I peered through the blur of rain, searching for a refuge. I heard the voice again: you must protect yourself from being struck by a falling—CRACK! A tree exploded in a flash of sparks and flying wood not ten feet from me and then I was running away from it, running in terror. And just when I thought I would collapse for certain I looked up through the trees and saw a door.

The cabin seemed to be growing right out of the rocks that rose behind it. I pounded on the door with my fist and then it fell open and I was inside. Dazed and dripping, I stood in a tiny room. I saw a table, a bench, a rug, a fire. I shut the door and though I could still hear the rain pelting on the roof, the space seemed mercifully quiet. Just for a moment, I thought, as I lay down on the rug and curled my body toward the comfort of the flames. Just until I'm warm....

When I awoke I realized there was a blanket covering me. I sat up and breathed in the smell of smoke, and food. Then I saw the girl. She had thick dark eyebrows and straight black hair. She was at the low table with her back to me, cutting something into small pieces. As I sat watching her she never stopped moving, or humming. She looked to be just about my age. When she turned toward the fire and saw that I was awake, she smiled and passed me a cup. It was bitter tea that made me cough, but spread warmth through my chest almost instantly.

"Who are you?" I asked, my voice catching in my throat and starting another coughing fit.

She kept on smiling and working, adding wood to the fire, sprinkling dried leaves in the pot.

"What is your name?" I said, once I thought my voice was close to normal.

The girl only gestured with her hand that I drink more, which I did, feeling warmer by the minute. Nevertheless, I clutched the rough blanket and pulled it tighter around my shoulders. I looked around the room. The rug I had been sleeping on was really a bearskin, with coarse black fur. The walls, too, were covered in animal skins, carefully scraped and stretched. In some places, patterns had been stitched or painted on them. There seemed to be only one small window next to the door, but it had no glass and was tightly shuttered against the weather. The only light came from the fire and a small lamp. I could hear that the rain was still falling, but it had slowed to a much gentler rate. There was no sound of wind, or thunder.

"Do you live here?" I asked her. No answer. She scooped something from the pot over the fire into a wooden bowl, then handed it to me with a spoon. I sat blowing on the steaming food, waiting for it to cool.

The girl pointed to herself and finally told me her name, "Marie-Madeleine."

I repeated, trying to say the unfamiliar syllables exactly as she had. She grinned. I ate a spoonful of the food she'd given me. Moose, I guessed, savouring its warmth and wild flavour.

I wondered if she had killed the animal herself. I noticed that she was wearing trousers held up with a piece of rope, and what looked like a man's shirt.

"*Et vous?*" she said, pointing to me.

"You're French!" I cried.

The girl frowned a little. She pointed to her chest. "Marie-Madeleine." Then she poked my chest. "*Et vous?*"

"Oh, sorry. My name is Elizabeth. Elizabeth." I pronounced each syllable with exaggerated emphasis. She said it back to me, ending with a clicking 't' instead of the proper sound, but it was close enough. I nodded, smiled, and cleaned out the bowl. It felt more normal to be with this strange girl in a tiny cabin far from civilization, than with the well-dressed girls from town on their picnic. I could feel my muscles relaxing, my heartbeat slowing, and my breath coming in a strong, steady rhythm.

I was just beginning to think about trying to get back home when the cabin door opened and a man stepped inside. He shook the rain from his silvery-black hair and put two pheasants on the table. Marie-Madeleine kissed him on the cheeks and they traded rapid phrases as the man hung up his coat.

It wasn't until he turned to warm his hands at the fire that he noticed me. I thought he would be startled, but he just stared at me, an uncanny calmness in his face. I tried to smile, though I'm sure my apprehension made it look more like a grimace.

Marie-Madeleine said something to the man and he continued staring at me. I guessed it was time to introduce myself so, clutching the blanket around me, I stood and reached out my hand. "Hello," I said. "My name is Elizabeth Evans."

As I spoke the words the man's face took on an expression as if I was forcing his hand into the flames. Then suddenly he was more terrible than the storm, knocking the cup and bowl onto the floor, tipping the table over with a crash.

He turned to Marie-Madeleine where she cringed, eyes shut tight, in the corner of the small room. "*Qu'est-ce qui se passe? Qu'est-ce que tu penses? Quand je pense à toutes les familles, perdues—perdues!—à cause des maudits Anglais. Jamais encore. Jamais!*"

When he turned back to me I cringed too.

"*Allez. Allez!*" he bellowed. I had no need to translate his words. His extended arm with one crooked finger pointing at the door gave me an unmistakable message.

Marie-Madeleine was pushing me gently but quickly to the doorway before I had a chance to say another word and then I was back outside. The door was shut behind me but I could still hear the man's voice echoing through the woods. The rain had stopped and the day was long over. I stumbled a few steps away from the cabin, then stood among the dripping trees, blinded by darkness and fear. The brook was my only route home and I had no idea where it was.

When I heard a cracking branch behind me, my rattled nerves made me jump and whirl around. Then I realized it was the girl. As she came close, she put out both hands, palms up, and shrugged. I nodded and took hold of one of her hands. I had known her only a few hours, but already I felt an alliance.

"Papa…" she began, but had nothing else to say.

I squeezed her hand, then pointed through the trees. "Help me find the brook," I said, adding a hand motion and a gurgling noise, the closest I could come to the sound of water running over rocks. She understood and took off like a rabbit along a twisty path. I did my best to follow, wishing I had trousers like hers. When we reached the brook we parted without another word, only smiles and a warm embrace. Somehow, I felt it was a beginning rather than an ending, even though I had no idea if I would ever see her again.

It wasn't until I saw our barns emerge from the darkness that I considered what sort of reaction might await me at the house. When I opened the kitchen door, Sadie nearly knocked me over with her hug, and then nearly knocked me over again with her chastisement.

"What do you have to say for yourself?" she demanded. "Here it is long past midnight and you're just gettin' home. Mr. Jefferson's gone out lookin' for you, sure that you were lost, or somethin' worse."

"I was lost," I insisted when I finally got a chance. "I was in the woods and a tree got hit by lightning and…" I knew then that I couldn't tell Sadie, or anyone else, about Marie-Madeleine. I should have given the girl full credit for saving me from my own foolishness and wet clothes, but I couldn't, not yet. Maybe it was the memory of Marie-Madeleine's father and his uncontrolled rage at the sound of my voice. Maybe it was the fact that their tiny cabin seemed deliberately hidden in the forest. Whatever my reason, I decided to keep my new friend a secret.

"What did you say?" Sadie said sharply.

"I said…I said I found a sheltered spot, a kind of cave under a big rock, and I slept there, on some boughs, and then I walked back when the storm was over." I tried to ignore the prickles of guilt I felt about lying to Sadie.

"Uh-huh," she said, looking at me hard for a moment. She apparently could find no reason to dispute me. She lifted the big pot from the fire and poured the hot water into the washtub. The steam swirled up and dampened her face. She wiped it dry with her apron. "Before you get in this bath you'd better try and catch Mr. Jefferson. He was going over to Lovetts' to raise a search party."

"Oh, no!" I ran outside, around the back of the garden fence and into the sloping field that lay between our property and Lovetts'. In the moonlight I could just see a small figure walking slowly along the edge of the woods, his head down, a light in one hand. I started to run but my legs trembled so that I almost fell. I called his name and he turned, waved the lantern, and began making his slow way back toward the house.

"Thank you for looking for me," I said as we came into the kitchen. "I'm sorry I caused you to worry." I made sure Sadie heard me as well.

"You, miss, need to get washed up and into bed. Mr. Jefferson's fed your cows hours ago." She shooed him out of the kitchen so I could use the water. As she helped me peel away my torn and muddy clothes she shook her head and made familiar scolding noises with her tongue.

In my bedroom, finally alone, I couldn't sleep. I picked up the diary from where it had rested since Mother had given it to me. I opened the cover and stared at the empty pages for a long time. Then I sat, dipped my pen, and wrote until my hand was numb. The book had finally found its subject.

By morning a strong west wind hurried little clouds across a brilliant blue sky. I worked beside Sadie tossing hay up onto the high-sided wagon where Mr. Jefferson spread the load. I thought about Marie-Madeleine and her father, remembering the conversations Father and I had had about the departure of the Acadian people. If they all left, I wondered, where did Marie-Madeleine come from and why were she and her father living in the woods behind our farm? I considered what Father would do if he knew about them. My mind was like the clouds, racing before the wind. He would probably insist that they pack up and leave, I thought. Perhaps I should forget I'd ever met them and then they could go on living in their cabin for as long as they needed to. I reasoned that their place was so far from anywhere no one else would notice it. Then I imagined Mr. Jefferson following a grouse through thick woods, carrying a gun.

I decided that the first thing I needed to do was find my new friend again, to see if I could help her in some way. I didn't know how I would accomplish it, but I knew I had to at least see her, to confirm that she was real and alive. In the meantime, I would work a lot harder at memorizing my French verbs.

Having made this decision, I was able to sit comfortably over supper with Sadie and Mr. Jefferson. We were all tired from our day's work, so there was little conversation. As I listened to the soft crackling of the embers in the kitchen fireplace, I thought of Marie-Madeleine's small cabin and the few possessions there. My house seemed to overflow with comforts.

Chapter Nine

❧

For the next few days I had no chance to search for my new friend. Sadie and I were too busy pickling beans. All I saw or seemed able to think about were the thin green fingers that we pulled from the plants by the dozens. And once they were picked and piled together in their baskets, they needed to have their ends snapped off before they could be cooked and packed in the jars. The smell of brine filled my head.

Finally, I found a morning when Sadie had no immediate need for me. I think she had taken pity on me, sensing my urge to be away from the house. She told me to go enjoy the fine morning and forget about beans for a few hours. I didn't have to be told more than once. I gathered up the few items I wanted to take with me: apple jelly left over from last year's batch, a small piece of butter, a square of cheese, a pair of shoes that were squeezing my toes but which I thought might fit Marie-Madeleine's feet, and, on a whim, the little cross that had been hidden in the corner of my writing desk since the picnic at Granville. I found the object comforting when I held it in the palm of my hand and let my fingers curl around the four points. Perhaps I can give some of that comfort to my friend, I thought.

The woods were cool and quiet. I stopped at the spot in the brook where I had been distracted by the lichen on that stormy afternoon. There, exactly where I had expected, was the grey rock face, showing itself as if it had burst through the moss and undergrowth for a breath of fresh air. I gripped the rock's gnarly surface as I climbed up and over it, then I struck off in the direction I felt certain was the right one. My confidence was unwavering and I began to anticipate the sight of the little cabin, smoke trailing from its stone chimney. I walked farther than I thought I needed to, then back to the rock, then set off in a new direction, and did the same thing all over again. But after three more tries I could still see no sign that any human but me had been in this part of the forest.

I was ready to give up when I spotted something that made my heart flutter. Hidden behind a dense clump of young spruce was the fallen tree. The tree that had drawn the lightning's force and had exploded so close to me. The tree, now fractured and gaping, whose violent end had sent me flying in terror, straight into the cabin door. I turned slowly around, straining my eyes to see what was hidden among the shadows of the forest. The greens and greys and browns, the rocks and trunks and bushes all began to blend together.

Perhaps they have gone, I thought, stricken by the notion that I would never see Marie-Madeleine again. Perhaps they gathered up their belongings and demolished the cabin, all because I found them.

I walked slowly back to the brook, my canvas satchel heavy across my shoulder and chest. Its contents banged and rattled annoyingly against my hip. I walked all the way home in a pitiful state. Nothing could draw me out of my despair.

Father returned from town and on Sunday we went to church together. I hardly said a word all the way. When I passed Charlotte in the churchyard I was sure she thought I was being terribly rude, but I had no will to converse about trivial matters. I was determined that I would find an answer to my mystery and where better to turn, I reasoned, in a quest for answers, than to God. If Marie-Madeleine exists, I prayed, then please let me know somehow. If she is out there, then help me find her. But if I see no sign, God, then I will turn my hands to work, I swear.

Nothing happened. I did as I had vowed and became devoted to work. Sadie, I think, was somewhat mystified, though she certainly didn't complain when I was in the kitchen before her with butter churned and bread already rising. By the end of the week, however, she was beginning to worry about my silent diligence.

"You're not yourself, I know it. Go out and get some fresh air, for heaven's sakes." She shooed me out the kitchen door. "And if you're looking for a chore, pick blackberries." She thrust a basket into my hands and shut the door firmly behind me.

The best berry patch was at the back of the cornfield, so I made my way along the familiar track with the tall cornstalks waving their golden fronds at me as I passed. I quickly lost myself in the tricky task of pulling the bumpy, purple-black berries from among their dangerous branches. My forearms were soon scratched and bloody, but it didn't bother me.

I had paused to slap a mosquito on the back of my neck when a sudden motion caught the edge of my eye. Too big for a bird, I thought, quickly scanning the trees. A bear? After the same sweet treasure as me, no doubt. I knew not to surprise her by staying quiet, so I began to sing the first thing that came into my head. "A mighty fortress is our God, a bulwark never failing...."

At the end of the first line, as I took a breath, I was sure I heard a giggle. Bears do not giggle, I thought. I shut my mouth tight and looked again into the woods, more carefully this time. I put the basket down. Silence. "Our helper he amid the flood…" my voice quavered, then grew more boisterous, "of mortal ills prevailing." I stopped. Laughter.

"Charlotte?" I couldn't imagine that she would have any reason for being in our woods. "Sadie?" She wasn't silly enough to play such a trick, much less giggle, I knew. I took a step or two in the direction I thought the laughter had come from. There was a distinct rustling sound and I saw a form crawling under the low branches of a spruce. In a flash I knew who the shape belonged to and my heart leaped.

"Marie-Madeleine!" I called out. "Is that you?" There was only silence and stillness in response. I felt like I was trying to make friends with a rabbit. Frustrated, I put my basket down. Then I had an idea. I popped a blackberry in my mouth. "Mmmm." I smacked my lips. There was more rustling in the branches. She sat up, a distance away, looking at me. I used a voice like the one I saved for new calves who were not yet used to human touch, whose nostrils flared when I tried to tie a lead on them. "Blackberry?" I ate another berry, then held out the basket.

She crawled slowly towards me until she was only a few feet away. She hesitated, looked into the basket at the nest of berries, then into my eyes with a questioning stare. I nodded vigorously and ate another berry, then stretched my arm out to hold the basket as close to her as I could. She grinned and reached into it.

"Blackberry," I said again, and then we sat down side by side at the edge of the woods where the tall trees met the tall corn and we ate every last berry I'd picked. When the basket was empty I wasn't sure what to do or say next. I determined that I would simply plunge in and see what we could make of it.

"*Où est ta maison?*" It came out rather slowly, but correctly, I thought.

Marie-Madeleine pointed into the woods and launched into a stream of words I could not recognize. I shook my head, pointed to myself and to her and then into the woods in the direction she had indicated. "Take me there? *Avec toi?*"

Marie-Madeleine's alarm was immediate. With wide eyes and flustered hands she said, "*Non, non.*" Then more gently, "*Papa....*" She bared her teeth and raised her hands up to make claws beside her hunched-up shoulders. The effect was unmistakable and I laughed. Then I clapped my hand over my mouth. The man was her father after all, and it was certainly not my intention to mock him. But Marie-Madeleine had started to laugh, too. She made the monster face again and I laughed again and soon we were both holding our sides with happy tears wetting our cheeks.

Once we'd calmed ourselves and caught our breath Marie-Madeleine pointed to me and said, "*Ta maison?*"

"My house? Oh, it's down there." I pointed in the direction of the cornfield. But that's ridiculous, I thought; she'll think I live in the corn. I pulled her by the arm to the corner of the field where the path led down the hill so we could see the roofs of the house and barn. "My house," I said. I thought I saw a look of admiration, perhaps even a little longing in her expression. It is rather impressive, I thought with pride, even if all she can see is the chimneys.

"We call it Evans Hall. Come with me." I tugged her arm, gesturing down the path, but she resisted and her eyes widened again.

"*Non, non.*" She was making the same hand-waving motions, this time more frantic. "*Papa m'a dit… jamais, jamais.*" Her voice sounded harsh and I shivered with the still-vivid memory of her father's angry words.

What we needed was a place to meet—a secret spot that would feel safe to Marie-Madeleine. Then I remembered. I scooped up my empty basket, gestured to her to follow me, and began to run along the edge of the trees. Marie-Madeleine was right behind me as I turned into the woods. I led her straight to the immense beech tree that shaded part of a large bed of ferns. I grabbed the lowest branch, swung myself up into the tree and settled on a broad, flat spot just big enough for two. Without a second's hesitation Marie-Madeleine swung herself up beside me. We grabbed each other's hands and held tight, smiling.

"Our house," I said, patting the branch and gripping her hand tighter. "*Chez nous.*" She nodded and I knew she understood. We would meet here again.

Two days passed before I had a chance, after supper, to slip away to the beech tree again. The wind had dropped down, the sun was low, and the air was full of golden light. I had brought my bag of treasures this time, knowing that if I didn't find my friend, I could at least leave the gifts in our tree.

There were no feet dangling from the broad beech branch, but I climbed up and settled myself, content to be quiet and patient for a time, hoping against hope that Marie-Madeleine might choose this same time to visit our place. I tried to prepare myself for disappointment.

After some time listening to the wind singing in the pine trees, I heard a different sound, a kind of buzzing screech. Then a dark head appeared below me and Marie-Madeleine tipped up her face. She held a long blade of grass between her thumbs, put it up to her lips and blew. The screeching buzz sounded again. I couldn't have counted the number of times I'd made the same noise myself.

"*Bonjour*! Oh, sorry. *Bon soir*," I said. She climbed the tree and I put the bag in her lap. "*C'est pour toi*." I was very proud of my new-found bravery with the French language. Marie-Madeleine burrowed into the satchel and her hand came out clutching the jelly. "Jelly," I said. "Apple jelly."

"Jelly?" Her letter 'j' was softer than mine.

I put a finger into the jar then into my mouth. Marie-Madeleine did the same, smiled, and wiped her chin with the back of her hand. Now this is the way to live, I thought. Who cares about gloves and pianos and handkerchiefs?

The butter and cheese brought a little more confusion than the jelly. "From my cows," I said as she held them. "Cows." I made finger horns and mooed just like Daisy but Marie-Madeleine didn't seem to understand. Even if she did live in the woods, I thought, surely she'd seen cows sometime. I wanted her to meet my cows in their sweet-smelling barn. I broke off a bite of cheese and gave it to her. She didn't need to know where it came from, just that it was delicious.

Next she pulled out the shoes and her comprehension was obvious. She tried them on, held her feet together and tapped them twice, then took them off again. I looked down at my own bare feet and wondered if the gift had been thoughtless. Why would she want shoes? Then I thought of their comfort

when the ground was frosty. I would have to bring stockings
the next time, I thought.

She felt around in the bottom of the bag for what
was left. Frowning a little, she unwrapped the white
handkerchief. When she exposed the cross she held it in her
palm for a long time. She touched the figure of Christ with
one finger. She curled her hand around the object just the
way I had done. When I looked at her face and saw tears
running down her cheeks, I thought for a moment that my
gift had achieved the opposite effect of the one I'd wished
for, that instead of giving her hope the cross might have
brought despair. But then she turned and hugged me, and I
knew it would be all right.

"*Je dois retourner chez moi,*" she said, and I noticed she spoke
slowly and clearly for me.

"*Chez toi?*" I returned, poking at her chest the way she had
done over the bowl of stew at our first meeting in her cabin.

"*Chez moi.*" She grinned and nodded. "*Toi aussi?*"

"*Oui.* I must go home."

"Home."

We both jumped from the branch.

"Tomorrow?" I searched for the right word. "*Demain?*"

"*Ah, oui, bien sûr. Demain.*" She patted the tree as if to say,
right here, same spot.

After another hug we turned our separate ways, Marie-Madeleine into the darkening forest, and I along the edge of the cornfield toward the setting sun and my comfortable bed.

When I had finished my goodnights, to Hazel and the cows, to Sadie and Mr. Jefferson, I went up to my room and pulled my diary from its hiding place. I looked at the little book and thought about the wonderful secret it now contained. It seemed as if I had found a magical friend, a forest fairy, or a nymph. Sometimes I had trouble convincing myself that Marie-Madeleine was real, except when I was with her. It was as if she was a ghost who was visible only to me.

The next evening, after I'd fed the cows, eaten supper, and crushed about a bushel of blackberries for jelly, I escaped and ran all the way to the beech tree. This time, my bag contained more cheese, some biscuits, a piece of gingerbread left over from supper, and a pair of stockings.

Marie-Madeleine was there before me, this time with a bag of her own. It looked like it was made of animal skin with a design like a quilt star on one side. When I looked closely I saw the design was made of porcupine quills. I'd seen similar work in Mr. Wolseley's store and knew it was from the Mi'kmaq women.

"*Pour toi*," she said as I was examining it. And then she reached inside and drew out a tiny basket box. Inside was a smooth white stone.

"*Merci*," I said, smiling. We sat quietly for a few minutes. I gathered my courage. "*Ton père…*" I said, struggling with a way to begin my questions. "Your family? *Ta famille?*"

"*Seulement moi et mon père et mon frère Jean. Il est…nous ne savons pas où.*"

"You have a brother!" I pictured a little boy with eyes as dark as hers. Then he changed into a strong young man, as angry and ferocious as their father. "You don't even know if he's alive?" I looked at her forlorn face. "*Toi et ton père chez vous.*"

"*Oui.*"

"*Et…ta mère?*" I said it in the gentlest voice possible, almost a whisper.

"*Ma mère? Elle est morte.*"

"Dead. Oh, I am sorry." I had known in my heart that she would tell me her mother was dead, but hearing her say it that way, so plainly, was unbearable. "How? *Comment?*"

"*Une fièvre.*"

I didn't understand and shook my head. She put the back of her hand on her forehead and rolled her eyes.

"Oh, a fever. She was ill."

"Ill?"

"Yes, ill, sick."

She looked down at her hands. "*Les autres aussi. Mes frères Jacques et Pierre, et ma soeur Gabrielle.*"

"You had a sister and two brothers? And they all died of
the same fever? That's horrible. Your poor father. And poor
you. You were just a baby, weren't you?" I was crying by then,
imagining the sorrowful scene. "But you are here. *Tu n'es pas
morte. Comment?*"

"*Nos amis ont amené des remèdes, des peaux.*"

Remèdes seemed obvious, but *peaux* I did not know. Perhaps
it was food, I thought. "*Peaux?*" I repeated.

She seemed at a loss for a moment, then made a motion
like wrapping a blanket around her shoulders. "*Des animaux.*"

"Oh, the skins of animals. Pelts. Of course." The Mi'kmaq
must have helped her family with remedies and clothes,
perhaps even sheltered them. But why not simply go to the
town? Why hide in the woods with only the natives to help
them? Especially with an infant, and feverish children, and
a dying wife. Why had this man, her father, risked the life
of his family so completely? He must have been a criminal, I
thought, and judging by what I had seen of his temper, quite a
dangerous one. Was Marie-Madeleine in any danger herself?

These questions were frustratingly complex for my scant
French. They would all have to wait. I realized it was getting
close to dark and I would be missed at home, so we parted
again with an agreement to meet the next evening. *Demain soir.*

Chapter Ten

All through the rest of the summer and into the early weeks of autumn we met when we could, when the ripening corn, or apples, or squash weren't taking up my time. If one of us visited the tree and didn't find the other, she would leave a clue or a treasure in a hollow place. It was a language of gifts.

I was amazed at how quickly Marie-Madeleine learned to understand and speak English. I had been having French lessons for years, but could barely navigate my tongue around a simple sentence. She picked up words and phrases easily and was soon able to express a surprising range of feelings and ideas. It felt odd to go from Evans Hall, where my father's English was carefully spoken in complete sentences, to the beech tree where all conversation was carried out in a loose and crazily jumbled mix, usually in fragments as they came to us. The latter seemed to me such a free and true form of expression that I became less and less interested in engaging in polite conversation with Father, or Mr. Jefferson, or our neighbours in the township.

On Sundays, of course, I spent part of the day going to service in town. No one did any farming on Sunday, and Sadie sat in her room reading the Bible. I often wondered, on those long quiet days, how Marie-Madeleine passed her holy days. She had shown me her *chapelet*, a string of beads that she explained were like counters—one for each prayer. She told me that the prayers were said to Mary, the mother of Jesus. Did she spend the day praying? Was Sunday any different than any other day when you had no church to go to?

I described for her the church at the old garrison in Annapolis, the wooden box pews with their little latched gates, the minister's grand pulpit, from which he expounded on the nature of faith, and sin, and community. I told her how his black robes flowed with his gestures and had the effect of hypnotizing my sleepy Sunday self so that by the end of his sermon I was in a trance, stunned by the words, and the light through the long windows, and the bobbing ribbons on the girls who sat in front of us. I was quite sure I achieved nothing of holiness and everything of sloth in church.

Mr. Jefferson, being Church of England himself, attended service with us and sat in our box. He held the gate for everyone else to enter first, like a farmer letting his sheep into the pen. Then he would find the appropriate page in his prayer book and follow the words of the liturgy with one calloused finger.

I tried to describe Mr. Jefferson to Marie-Madeleine, but every time I did I got more and more confused. She must have thought that I liked him one day and hated him the next.

"Is he a good man, like your father?" she asked.

"I think he is," I told her. "Even though I don't want to admit it. He does a good job at whatever tasks Father gives him." I didn't say anything about fishing.

One evening, with a fresh apple in my hand and the golden-green of the cornfield glowing in the low sunlight, I sat in the tree reading a letter from Mother. When Marie-Madeleine climbed up she asked why I was frowning.

"My mother," I said, waving the letter. "She is determined to find a husband for me. I can't seem to convince her that I don't need one. She keeps writing to me about this man and that man and how suitable they would be. I wish she would listen to me instead of constantly nagging."

Marie-Madeleine was silent.

"Oh, I'm so sorry," I sighed. "It was thoughtless of me to complain about my mother when you.... *Je regrette de t'avoir blessée.*"

She shrugged. "I did not know my mother. You tell me about yours."

"Oh, she tells everyone what to do. *Tout le temps*. And she talks too much. And she is always complaining about how difficult life is here—how there is no proper silversmith, and no decent school, and goods are too expensive, and she doesn't like the weather. I like it better when she's gone. At least then I can put away her words and not listen." I made an elaborate show of folding the pages of the letter over and over and stuffing it into my pocket. I knew Marie-Madeleine had probably understood little of my tirade, but it felt good to speak it and the September air seemed clearer afterwards.

Sometimes Marie-Madeleine told stories from her life—a dream she'd had, an animal or bird she'd encountered in the woods. One day she described, with a mixture of words and actions, a Mi'kmaq ceremony she and her father had attended. There had been drumming, and dancing, and a feast of salmon and berries. The way her face looked as she told me the story made me wonder if these people were like family for her. They had probably saved her life, and had been her only community, her only source of information about the rest of the world. I wondered if that made Marie-Madeleine a savage, the word so many townspeople used.

Sometimes she told stories that had come from her father, about the family's life before, when they lived at the edge of the forest, near the river, and had animals, and played music and danced with their neighbours. But she would never tell what had happened to change all that, and I could never find the right way to ask her. It was an invisible barrier in our conversations.

Questions bubbled in my mind, troubling me as I went about my chores. Why had her family stayed behind when the others left? Was it because her mother was about to have a baby? Was it illness that had forced them to stay when their neighbours had decided to leave?

From time to time, as our friendship grew stronger, I would try to convince Marie-Madeleine to come home with me, but she always refused with a forcefulness that left no room for argument. The beech tree was enough of a test of her confidence in me, and I could not persuade her to venture any farther down the mountain. So we shared a twilight world, suspended between solid ground and sky, between her tongue and mine, each understanding only a part of the other's words, neither asking for anything but warm companionship.

Once, when we had lingered long enough to see the first star twinkle white against the deep purple sky, I asked if she had ever wished on the first star of evening.

Marie-Madeleine laughed and said, "What do you wish for?"

I jumped down from the branch and looked up at her. "I wish no one would tell me I had to have a husband, or wear dresses, or go to church, or play the piano. And I wish to live on my own farm and raise crops and animals for as long as I can." That is what I've wished for all along, I thought. "*Et toi?*" I expected her to say she wished to have her family back.

"*Mon voeu,*" she said slowly, looking at the star. She let herself drop from the branch into the pale leaves of the dead ferns. "I wish to be a farmer with you."

I watched her walk away until she disappeared into the black forest.

Sadie and I spent the next five days picking the last of the apples, pressing the bruised ones into cider, making pies, and drying others for winter. Mr. Jefferson and the neighbours helped one another harvest the other crops. Most of the yield was sold and sent to Halifax to supply the hungry troops that were, according to what Father read to us from his newspapers, gathering thicker by the week.

Once that work was finished, Mr. Jefferson turned his attention to his scheme to clear more land on the hills. He took advantage of help from the Bencroft boys, agreeing to give them some of the logs for the new barn they were building.

Sadie made me take dinner up to the workers every day and as their labour progressed, the scene that met my eyes at the edge of the new field was more and more dismal. Smouldering piles of brush, bent and broken trees, overturned roots, and huge gaping holes were soon all that remained of a section of quiet forest.

One day, as I arrived with the basket at noon, Mr. Jefferson came toward me, leading Hazel. She was covered in sweat. I reached out to stroke her neck when she was close enough.

"I think she's limping a little." I raised Hazel's front hoof, searching for a caught stone or a sign of injury. "You've been working her awfully hard. This is a job for oxen, not a horse." I looked across the clearing to where the Bencrofts' yoked team strained to drag out another enormous stump.

"Don't worry. We just use her for moving the logs." He took a long drink from the water pail. "We're making good progress, don't you think?"

I gave Hazel the apple I'd brought for her. "I suppose."

"I'm not used to all these trees, myself."

"No trees in Yorkshire?"

He took another drink, then splashed some water on his face and neck. His hands were dark with pitch. "Hardly a one," he said. "It's all bare hills and stone fences."

"Aren't you sorry to be cutting all these down?" I really wanted him to be sorry, to feel regret.

"No." He dried his face on the sleeve of his shirt. "This'll make a good field for oats. Just wait."

As much as the angry scar on the land pained me, I couldn't help but admire his determination. Would I have the same energy if I faced an unfamiliar obstacle? I wondered. Would I be able to learn the skills necessary to build a whole new place, or was I completely dependent on the ready-made farm I expected my father to pass on to me?

The other men had begun to gather around, hungry for their dinner. They joked and teased each other easily and wiped the grime from their faces. "Thank you, Miss Evans," I heard them calling out as I walked away. I was glad to be free of the sight of such destruction. It was a grim reminder of the fragility of Marie-Madeleine's claim on the forest.

The next day Father brought home a letter saying that Mother was returning. My time would once again be shadowed by her wishes, her demands, her objections. I tidied my room and helped Sadie prepare the rest of the house to meet Mother's standards, and then we waited.

Less than a week after the letter, Mother's ship arrived and she swept back into the household, full of news about how dreadfully people were behaving in New England, and how concerned her brothers and sisters were for their sons who had enlisted in General Washington's army. She chattered on about her brother's career and the various cousins she'd visited, the varieties of cakes she'd been offered at this card party or that concert. I pretended to listen and put away her clothing and belongings as instructed, all the time waiting for her to bring up the promises Father and I had made in the spring.

"You've changed, Elizabeth," she said as I brought her tea to the sitting room once we had finally unpacked to her satisfaction.

"Surely you won't say I've grown, Mother," I said. I stood in front of her, waiting for a comment about my hair, or my hands, or my freckles.

"No, no." She looked at me with a searching curiosity I found surprising. "I suppose you're a woman, more than a girl now." And that was the end of it. No questions about the dresses or the diary. She seemed preoccupied, somehow. I had expected her to be sad about leaving Massachusetts again, but there was a vacancy about her face and manner, as if her mind was still aboard the ship, as if she had come home in body only.

On the Sunday after Mother's return I sat next to Charlotte at church. I was apologizing for being such a neglectful instructor and friend over the autumn, but she was quick to forgive.

"I understand, Miss Elizabeth," she said behind her glove. "I can't imagine how you pick all those apples in your orchards, and make the cider and all the other chores you have at this time of year. We know so little of it here in town, I always feel guilty."

I should feel guilty, I thought, for hiding my secrets and forgetting my obligations.

As the parishioners settled themselves, Charlotte continued, her whispered words near my ear mingling with the shuffling of feet and rustling of skirts. "Did you hear about that band of people who came through town last week? Oh, my, Elizabeth, you should have seen them. It was pitiful. They were dressed in rags and their hair was so tangled and long, and most of them were in bare feet."

"Who were they?" I opened my prayer book and began turning pages, occupying my hands.

"I don't know. Some French people. At least I think I heard them speaking French. Though not many of them said anything at all, just walked slowly down the street. Like they were sleeping. And their oxen were so thin I thought they might fall dead at any moment."

"Where had they come from?" She had my full attention, though I still pretended to be more interested in the prayer book.

"Mr. Wolseley told me he'd heard they had walked all the way from Boston. Imagine!"

"Where were they headed?" I whispered. Mr. Rice took his place at the lectern and stood glowering over his congregation.

"I don't know. They certainly weren't stopping in town, and a good thing, too. I don't think anyone would have given them any place to stay. They were so unpleasant. Worse than Gypsies, Mr. Wolseley said."

Mother's sharp elbow found my ribs as Mr. Rice cleared his throat and began the lesson. All through the service I could hardly keep still, thinking about when I could next see Marie-Madeleine and tell her about the travellers.

My urgency was frustrated by the autumn ritual I liked least. That night at supper Father and Mr. Jefferson declared that the next morning they would slaughter the pig. By the time the sun was over the top of the mountain the poor beast was dead, and was hanging from a large tripod they had erected in the yard. Sadie and I dragged out our biggest iron pot for the task of collecting all the fat for tallow.

Watching Mr. Jefferson haul the bloody carcass up I thought of the labours that would follow this death. Aside from the meat itself which, though messy, was dispensed with fairly quickly, the pig's body represented a significant portion of our household products. Sadie would have the worst of it, mixing the tallow with the lye she'd made from saved ashes to make her strong, smelly soap. I had been in charge of making the candles since I was big enough to hold the ladle that poured hot tallow into the moulds. For this day, however, all we considered was meat and blood and bone.

In the morning, while we sat over a breakfast of pork scraps sizzling from the pan and biscuits for soaking up the grease, a furious knocking at the kitchen door startled us.

"Colonel Evans, sir," a boy's voice called out. Father opened the door and in fell Samuel Bencroft, puffing and scared. "Colonel Evans, a bear's got one of our sheep!" He could barely get the words out before Mr. Jefferson had taken the gun and powder horn down from the wall. "Father and Mr. Hardy is goin' out to hunt it down," Samuel continued. "They want any men who can help."

Father was putting on his coat, but Mother grabbed his arm. "Henry, surely you don't intend to go out with them."

He shook her off, and said, "I most certainly do. Samuel's father helped me build this house and I have looked for ways to help him ever since. Now you women will stay inside until the beast is found." The wind slammed the door shut behind him.

The kitchen was silent until Mother's voice broke the spell. "This is what we get for living in such a godforsaken place." She went to the sitting room.

Sadie and I cleared away the remains of breakfast without speaking. I worked at hackling flax for most of the day, drawing the dried plants through the spikes of the hackle until all the useless, short fibres had fallen away and all that remained were the long, silky strands. By afternoon my fingers were raw and sore.

Father and Mr. Jefferson returned in the dark, exhausted and hungry. They had seen no bear.

The next morning, a few hours after their departure into a drizzly dawn, they came back with the news that Mr. Bencroft had shot the bear and the livestock were now safe. I hung their wet leggings by the fire. The black fur I'd slept on in Marie-Madeleine's cabin was still a vivid memory.

"We don't usually have to worry about bears," Father said as he spread a generous dose of molasses on a piece of cornbread. "They are generally quite timid and avoid humans, unless we threaten their cubs somehow."

"Wasn't as big as I expected." That was the extent of Mr. Jefferson's comments on the subject. He continued cleaning the gun, even though it had not been fired. I noticed how precisely his long fingers handled the weapon, and how carefully he inspected each piece as he reassembled it. I wondered if he was disappointed that he hadn't managed to kill the bear himself.

By afternoon, the drizzle had turned into steady, cold rain and the wind blew the smoke down the chimneys. I found Father in his study. He sat at his desk and I watched him sign his name to the bottom of a letter, set it aside, then pull out a fresh sheet and begin another.

"Father?"

"Hmm?" He hardly paused.

I settled into the chair by the fire. "Do you remember that you told me the Acadian people were all gone?"

He lifted his quill from the page and looked at me. "Yes, I said that most of them went back to France, where their families had come from."

"But did they all leave? I mean, didn't some families stay behind?"

"Well, there were those who chose to take the oath and demonstrate their loyalty to the Crown, but very few." He dipped his pen and began again.

I waited for a moment, listening to the scratch of metal nib on paper. When Father's hand reached for the ink bottle again, I said, "Were there any who tried to stay and avoid the oath?"

This time he put his pen down and folded his hands,

resting his elbows on the desk. "Well, yes," he said, "there were some rebels who carried out raids in collusion with the Mi'kmaq, and that is why we needed the militia in those early years. In my role as colonel I planned defences for the township should those violent factions have caused any further trouble for the settlement."

"Violent factions…." I imagined Marie-Madeleine's father in a fierce battle with my father's militia. "But that conflict is all over, is it not? The British control of the territory is secure." I paused to listen for his argument, but he had picked up his pen again. I allowed my curiosity another step. "Is the government allowing some Acadians to return?" I asked.

"How did you come to hear about this?" He put aside another finished letter.

"Charlotte said a group of French people were seen passing through town not long ago, and that they had walked all the way from Boston."

Father showed no surprise. "They're not the first to do so. Groups of them have been arriving over the years, to take up farming and fishing on St. Mary's Bay where the government has generously allowed them to resettle."

"So any French people still living here would be free to join them."

"Any living here have been captured or were driven out by the militia years ago." He sounded mildly offended, as if I had insulted his military efforts.

"Oh." I couldn't tell him that I knew he was wrong. Not yet.

"Why are you asking these questions, Elizabeth?" He jabbed at the ink bottle.

"Oh, no reason, really." I searched quickly for an explanation. "I saw an old foundation over in Granville in the summer, with Charlotte and her friends, and I was just thinking about that spot and wondering how we would feel if for some reason we had to leave our farm and then we came back years later and it was all gone."

"You sound like a little girl again, Elizabeth," he smiled. "You always did let yourself get so drawn into these stories." He shook his head, then turned back to his letters, apparently satisfied with my answer and with his own capacity to dismiss my mental wanderings as the whims of a foolish girl.

I was about to leave the room when he spoke again. "I forgot to tell you. Mr. Bencroft informed me that his oldest son is to be married soon. The bride will be coming to live at their farm in the spring."

"I pity the poor girl, having to listen to Mrs. Bencroft every day."

"Don't be rude, Elizabeth." He tidied up the stack of letters and put them to one side. Then he turned to face me. "I am proud that you want to run the farm some day and I fully intend to make it legally yours in my will, but there is one thing I want you to consider."

"What is it?"

"Sadie and I won't be here to help you forever. You need a partner, someone you can trust and respect. And also," he blushed a little and I almost laughed out loud, wondering what he would say next, "it would give me joy to watch my grandchildren grow up here on the farm."

In all of Mother's nagging about husbands she had never said anything that affected me the way Father's words did. I always said I didn't need a husband to run a farm, but he had introduced the one compelling reason to consider finding one. What good would it be for me to maintain the farm if there was no generation of the family to come? I couldn't find any response and my voice would have broken if I'd tried, so I just hugged him and left the room.

Chapter Eleven

❧

Though the sky was no longer the deep blue of October, the air was soft and the sun warmed our heads as Sadie and I took pickles, wine, and half a dozen pumpkin pies to the church where long tables had been set up for a community Thanksgiving supper. Mr. Rice's blessing on the feast was overlong and some of the dishes had cooled too much by the time we all sat, but it was a merry party, and a grateful end to a good season.

The following day was more typical of November—raw and grey, with the smell of snow in the air. My head felt odd and there was an unfamiliar stiffness in my limbs, but I tried to ignore it. Mr. Jefferson was taking the day off from clearing and had gone into town with Father. Mother was suffering with a head cold and she went back to bed right after breakfast. I packed a basket with some food left over from the night before, and headed up the hill to the beech tree. I took a book and a blanket, too, determined to stay until I could share Charlotte's story with Marie-Madeleine.

The wind was up, so I sat on the ground, sheltered by the wide trunk. I tried to concentrate on reading, but my mind kept returning to the image of women and their babies, children, and fathers walking for weeks in dense forests, their ox carts straining through the swamps and over the mountains. How many times had the axles broken? How many times had they been forced to pause for bad weather or illness? How many had they buried along the way? I wasn't convinced that a few parcels of rough land on St. Mary's Bay were worth months of agony.

I dozed off, my head swirling with these endless questions. When I opened my eyes Marie-Madeleine was sitting on the ground near me, eating a piece of apple pie with her fingers. I told her, in the words I could think of, about Charlotte's encounter.

"*Je sais*," she said calmly, her mouth full of pie. "My father saw them. *Il a trouvé ses cousins.*"

"Cousins! That's wonderful. He must be so happy." Then my heart sank. "Oh, this means you will be leaving, will you? *Vous partez?*"

"*Non*. His cousin say we can go live with them and fish, but my father refuse to go. He think the governor is trying to trick us. I think he is not right in the head anymore. This is what he was waiting for—the return of *les exilés*."

"Exiles?" The word had no real meaning for me. I said it again, feeling it slip past my tongue and across my teeth. A few snowflakes drifted down through the branches of the tree. "I don't understand," I said finally. "Why would they come all this way? What is so important?"

"*Acadie*." She said the one word and closed her eyes. When she opened them again, she said, "Papa told me he always knew they would come back. This is our place. Our home. This is where we are who we are. But now he has been too long afraid. Hiding. He doesn't know how to…." She stopped, and looked out at the grey river, and the snow clouds. Then she spoke again and her voice was changed. She sounded like an old, old woman. I knew she was telling me the story I'd been waiting to hear, the one her father must have told again and again, so many times it was burned into her mind, as if she had witnessed it with her own eyes. It had become part of her blood, her very essence.

As she spoke I saw the smoke from dozens of fires streaming across trampled fields. There were soldiers with uniforms and rifles, pushing and shouting at women clutching their bundles, their children. I heard the screaming, felt the panic, the exhaustion, the agony. She described the ships the people were forced to board, families separated, watching their houses and barns burn away and their own destinies dissolve like the ashes that landed on the muddy waters of the basin. And the emptiness when it was all over. The terrible silence that Marie-Madeleine's parents must have heard from their hiding place as they struggled to keep the little ones quiet. I thought of the baby, kicking in her mother's belly as she waited to be born into a world that would not welcome her.

There was nothing I could say when she had finished. I wanted to tell her I was sorry, but I knew it could never be enough, so I said nothing, only held her hand. After we parted, I stumbled home, the snowflakes flying around me as if they were afraid to land. My eyes were blurry from crying. With every step my feet took down the familiar pathways and across the frozen fields, I felt a growing heaviness in every limb. My head pounded.

Evans Hall, when I reached it, was empty and cold. I didn't bother to build up the fires but went upstairs to my room and fell into the chair. I believed now, with certainty, that the little cross in Marie-Madeleine's pocket had been dropped from a terrified hand and left for years in the ruins of a house. A message from a ghost. I shuddered and stared at the wall, seeing shapes and shadows that were not there.

Eventually, I became aware of Sadie's presence, and her voice. She hustled me into the bed and covered me with all the quilts. After a while she returned with some broth, which I know she fed me but I didn't taste. When she covered me up again I fell into a restless and frightening sleep. Voices cried through smoky fields and grey water splashed around my feet.

The next time I recognized Sadie she was opening my curtains. Sunlight streamed in. Afternoon, I thought.

She crossed to the bed and felt my forehead. "That's better."

I began to turn back the covers but she stopped me with a firm hand.

"You're staying right there."

"But I'm fine. I've had a long sleep and I'm fine."

"You are not. You've just come out of a bad fever. Miss Charlotte's had the same thing and the doctor's been at their place three times. Her father was sure she would die. I sent your mother to Lovetts' so she wouldn't catch it too." She tucked the quilts firmly around my body. "Even if you did get out of bed you wouldn't be able to stand up. You haven't eaten anything but broth for three days."

Three days. My mind searched for its last memory, groping through the fog. Marie-Madeleine. Was it real? Was her story true, or had I dreamed it all? Had I given her the fever, was she lying in the cabin, ill and afraid to die like her brothers and sister?

"Are you hungry?" Sadie's voice pulled me back to the sun-filled room.

I thought about it for a moment, feeling my body where it lay under the heavy quilts. An emptiness in my belly seemed to be asking to be filled. "Yes."

She brought me a thin slice of bread and a little cheese. I chewed slowly and lay back against the pillows looking at the shadows of the tree branches where they danced on the ceiling. The sun was low and the room seemed to glow with its peculiar orange light. I tried to think, to find answers in the confusion, but I was too tired. I put the plate aside, closed my eyes, and slept again.

The next day, I convinced Sadie to let me get up. I would suffocate otherwise, I told her. I needed to feel the floor under my feet before I could sort out my thoughts. As I passed through the hall and down the stairs, running my hand along the oak banister as I always did, I felt like I was walking through a dream. Evans Hall was exactly the same in every detail, and yet it felt like a place I had never lived. I was a stranger, lost, uncertain of which way to turn.

I paused beside the closed study door. A memory came to me, an image of Father lighting his pipe, the smoke coiling around his head. How could I have believed his stories? How could I ever have imagined they walked away by choice? Father would never admit that our prosperity was not our own doing. We had stolen it from them. And we had given them nothing in return. Less than nothing.

I stumbled to the kitchen. Mr. Jefferson was finishing his breakfast.

"Feeling better?" he asked.

I couldn't answer, but sat down across from him with my back to the fire. My shoulders ached as if I had carried a heavy burden through the night.

He poured tea into a cup and slid it across the table to me. I reached for a warm biscuit, then sat staring at it, unable to bring myself to take a bite. It was the same kind of biscuit Sadie had always made for us, but on that morning it was an unfamiliar lump. A dull throbbing filled my head.

Mr. Jefferson stayed at the table even though there was nothing left on his plate. "It was a good harvest this year. Next year will be even bigger, I'm sure of it."

I couldn't tell if he was making conversation or reciting a speech.

"In Yorkshire I never saw a farm as fine as this one." His smile was wide, and seemed more private than shared.

How smug he is, I thought. What does he know about how

those fields came to be so fertile, about how the orchards grew so fruitful? How dare he take such satisfaction from my farm?

My farm. The thought struck me like a blow to the chest. Oh, no. Not my farm at all. Not at all.

I must have made some sound because Mr. Jefferson was now looking at me and frowning. "Miss Evans, are you all right?" He stood up. "Shall I get Sadie? You're so pale."

I shook myself free from the invisible icy hands that gripped me and rose from the table. "No. No. Don't bother." Still holding the thick shawl Sadie had put on my shoulders, I walked through the house without seeing it, straight out the front door and down the hill toward the orchard. I heard my name called, but kept on walking. Then I felt Father's hands on my shoulders. He turned me around and held me to his side as we walked back to the house. He took me straight into his study, sat me in the big chair by the fire, and tucked my shawl around me. Then he poured a glass of brandy and handed it to me. When I hesitated he folded his arms across his chest and glared down at me. "Drink."

As the liquid burned in my throat, I found my voice again. "How could you?" I choked out. "How could you?"

"What is it? What have I done now?"

"I believed everything you told me," I said, looking at him

as if for the first time. "I believed this was our true home, that we belonged here, that it was rightfully ours. You made me believe that no one suffered, that it was a choice. But now I know. Now I know what's true."

"You are feverish again, Elizabeth. Delirious."

"I am not! I finally see everything clearly. The only reason we ever came here, the only reason the government offered us this land, was to keep the others away. They drove them out, then brought us in to fill the gap, to leave no room for return. We don't belong here. This is not our place. Why didn't you ever tell me? Why did you keep it from me?" For once I didn't cry. Bitterness had dried up all my tears.

Father turned his face to the window, as if a movement outside had caught his attention. I stared at him, struggling to get my breath back to normal, willing him to look at me, to speak.

He managed to control his voice, but still he kept his gaze turned away. "The land was empty when we arrived," he said slowly. "It was too beautiful to believe. Orchards, fields, dykes. We took the grants knowing our families could prosper here, believing the others would never return. We'd heard stories of the deportation, of course. Some of the men I'd met were soldiers who'd been part of it. Yes, they forced people onto ships." Here he paused and finally looked at me. "Everyone believed it was necessary. They are French. We are English. Our empires were at war."

His words seemed too loud for my ears and I put my hands over them, trying to muffle the sound. Marie-Madeleine was no empire, just a girl like me. But I had been protected all my life, sheltered. I had chosen to be satisfied with Father's explanations. There was a feeling like a plucked string between my ribs, a sharp twinge, and then the pain subsided.

Father was studying my face. "What happened to you, Elizabeth?"

"I found someone…." I hesitated. "A girl, in the woods." I told him about Marie-Madeleine and her father. Not the whole story, but enough for him to understand that I wasn't imagining it. "And you have to promise me you will tell no one about her. They are still afraid, still hiding. You have to promise to keep the secret."

"I promise," he said solemnly.

I returned to my bed, not caring who came or went. I heard doors opening and closing, voices at the bottom of the stairs, drifting up from the sitting room. Mother returned, when the danger of illness had passed, and she fussed over me a little. When Charlotte's father visited she tried to persuade me to see him, but I refused. He must have assumed I was suffering the same effects as Charlotte when Mother told him I was unable to see visitors. I did ask her to give Mr. Rice a note that I scribbled to Charlotte saying that I was looking forward to resuming our lessons as soon as she was able. It was not true.

In the failing afternoon light of a day whose name I could not find, Mother came into my room, knocking softly as she opened the door. I waited for the scolding, the worrying words, the chatter about things I needed to be strong for. She sat down on the edge of the bed.

"You are no longer sick, are you?" She said it so plainly that I blurted the truth without trying to hide it.

"No, I'm not."

"Then you will tell me today what is troubling you so we can do something about it."

"It's nothing, Mother."

"Is it Mr. Jefferson? Has he said something, done something?" Her dark look startled me. "Has he...offended you?"

"No more than usual."

"Are you certain? You can tell me the truth, my dear, and your father will send him away, no matter how useful he is, if he has hurt you in any way." She was holding my hand now, and reaching for a handkerchief.

I hesitated, seeing in an instant an easy way to rid our farm of the ambitious Mr. Jefferson, but I shook my head. He was now the least of my troubles. "No, Mother. Honestly, he has done nothing to hurt me."

She heaved a tremendous sigh of relief and put the handkerchief away. Then her face changed again, the softness disappearing. "Frankly, Elizabeth, I'm at a loss. If you are not sick, and you won't tell me what's bothering you, how can I help?" She paused, searching my eyes.

"Please, Mother, just leave me alone. I have nothing to tell you."

In the middle of the night I awoke from a dream. I had been in a schoolhouse, standing at the front of the room. Rows of small faces looked up at me, waiting. I tried to speak, but my mouth wouldn't open. It felt as if it was sealed shut, like a bolted door. It terrified me.

I got out of bed and found my shawl. Pulling it around me I went quietly down the stairs and into the kitchen. Embers, nearly dead, sizzled in the fireplace. I put some small sticks on and blew to raise a flame, then stayed crouched on the floor as the fire took hold and grew brighter.

How can I go on living here? I asked myself. How can I look down from my windows at the orchard, at the marsh fields, and feel anything but shame? I don't belong here any more than Mother does, I thought, my heart sinking at the notion. At least Mother knew there was a place she

could call home, even if she couldn't be there. I was left with
nothing to yearn for. My only happiness was in ignorance,
and now that it was gone, there was no reason to wish it
back again.

After the flames had faded to embers again, I climbed
back up the stairs, carrying a candle. Before returning to bed
I pulled the diary from my desk and held the candle over
its thin pages to read the words I had written. I wondered if
Mother ever wanted to unlearn the lessons that led to her life
as a woman, a wife, a mother.

An idea came into my mind then, not with a flash, but more
like snow slowly covering the ground, turning dull, lifeless
brown into clean white. I heard myself murmur the words of my
decision. "I have to leave Annapolis," I said into the darkness.
It was the only way. I would go to Sudbury with Mother. Mr.
Jefferson could have the farm, with Father's blessing.

After breakfast I followed Mother to the sitting room and
repeated my nighttime declaration. She said nothing, but sat
staring at me. "I said, I have to leave. I'm ready to go and live
with Uncle William. I'll help in his school, or take care of his
children, whatever is necessary."

Mother's face twisted. I could see the conflict that must
have been raging inside her. Part of her wanted to celebrate
my decision, and part of her was troubled. "Well," she said,

controlling her voice, "this is a surprise. I don't understand. In the spring you were so definite."

"I've had a change of heart." How true, I thought. The words described my situation precisely. My heart had been changed forever. Everything I held dear, everything I had been so content with, so sure of, was shaken to pieces, and all that remained was a knowledge that I no longer belonged at Evans Hall. I had to leave as soon as possible. "Could we go before Christmas?"

"Heavens no, dear. No, let us wait until the sailing is good and perhaps by then the turmoil in Boston will have subsided. I don't want to take my daughter to a place where they burn effigies of King George in the public squares nearly every day of the week and where those awful soldiers bully decent citizens." She picked up her needlework and began making tiny stitches. "Peace will be restored by spring, one way or another, and you and I can finally go together to stay for as long as you like. William and Lydia will be thrilled."

I didn't bother to tell her that I had no plan to return. "Please don't tell Sadie," I begged. "I'll do it myself." I couldn't imagine where I would find the courage.

"Very well," she said. "We can share your news with your father together. He may be a little sad at first, but he'll know this is for the best. He will understand, don't worry."

I knew Father would understand, all too well. His eyes, across the supper table, were difficult to look at, but I could feel neither sympathy nor satisfaction. Betrayal and sorrow had taken over and there was room in me for no other emotions.

Chapter Twelve

The daylight hours shrank until the world was a dark cave. Every time I lit a candle I thought back to the day I had dipped a winter's worth of tallow. It felt like years had passed since then. I tried to picture Marie-Madeleine's face, but as one detail would come into focus, the others would slip away. Visiting the beech tree was unthinkable. I could barely muster the strength to carry out my normal chores. The notion of trying to walk all that way was overwhelming.

Sadie put me to work spinning, since it was a job I could do sitting down. The humming rhythm of the wheel lulled me into a state of forgetfulness that I found easy. I pictured her weaving it all into the warm linsey-woolsey cloth we used for nearly everything we wore.

I could hardly bear to go outside. Looking out at the familiar fields with my new, changed eyes was too painful. Some days, though, I could no longer stand the kitchen smoke and the boredom and I escaped outdoors to walk a little, just to get fresh air into my body. Whenever I heard a gunshot rolling down off the mountain I cringed, worrying that Mr. Jefferson would stumble upon Marie-Madeleine's cabin. But there was nothing I could do.

One afternoon, the sounds of Mother's card party filled every corner of the house. Mrs. Lovett was there, of course, and Mrs. Bencroft, whose voice was like a church bell sounding over and over. Mrs. Winniett was more like a sparrow, tiny and chirping. I had only ever seen her eat the crumbs from her plate. They all talked at once and I wondered how they ever heard each other, or got through a whole card game. I was sure Mother would insist that I play the piano for them, but she didn't. Either she was too excited by news of a wedding, or I was too good at hiding. But even in my room with the door shut and the quilts over my head, I was sure the sound of their voices would grind me to dust.

I finally left the house without being seen and walked down through the orchard under the swoop of the bare apple tree branches. Each limb seemed to reach out to grab me. I ran through them and out onto the marsh, farther from the house than I had been since my illness. Away from the trees, the cold air bit my face and ears. All around me I saw no colour, no life. I stood facing the river, letting the wind pummel me with all its strength. It seemed to reach right through me, to blow through my bones.

When I turned back to the house I felt lighter, as if the wind had blown away some chaff within me. I knew then that I could get through the winter, that I had enough labour to occupy me, and that when spring came I would be free to begin my life again. What that life would feel like, I had no idea.

We were well into December before Mr. Jefferson finally killed the moose he had stalked for a solid week. Sadie and I shared the task of cutting up the meat while Mr. Jefferson slept away his exhaustion. When he came downstairs to the kitchen, Sadie said to him, "Mr. Jefferson, you'll take Elizabeth in the sleigh to give some of this meat to Mrs. Spencer."

He looked at me, as if I might confirm or deny the order, but I kept my face still. "I'll get Hazel ready," he said.

There was just enough snow for the sleigh to run smoothly and more was falling from a grey sky. We travelled in silence down over the hill to Sawmill Creek and along to Mrs. Spencer's house. Mr. Jefferson spoke quietly to Hazel and she ran easily under his hands.

Mercy opened the door with the baby on her shoulder. I could see the little ones peeking out from behind her. When they recognized me, they came rushing out and wrapped their arms around my legs, looking up at me with pale, grinning faces.

"Where's your mother?" I asked Mercy.

"She's layin' down. Don't feel well." She pointed to the sitting room.

"Is she sleeping?"

Mercy shrugged. I put the parcel of meat of the table. "Do you know how to roast moose meat? Or make a stew?" She nodded.

In the sitting room I found Mrs. Spencer on the bed. Her face was white and her knuckles too. She gripped the top of the quilt, curling it up in her fists. Beads of sweat had formed along the lines of her forehead. Her eyes were squeezed shut.

"Oh, Miss Evans," she said when she opened her eyes and noticed me. Her voice was barely a whisper.

"I'm sorry to hear you've been unwell, Mrs. Spencer." I said the words through tight lips, afraid of what might happen if I breathed in too much of the room's horrible air.

"It's nothing, dear. It'll pass. Always does." She swallowed, with difficulty. "Pain's bad now, though. Worse than last year, with the baby. You remember?"

I nodded dumbly. She grimaced again, gasping as she pulled at the quilt. Her face had gone grey. I looked down at my useless hands. The urge to run from the room was strong, but there seemed to be no blood flowing through my body.

I had witnessed agony in that room before, the night the

baby was born. The house had been filled with a sense of hope. This time, it was all darkness, pain, and despair.

I found my voice and managed to speak again. "Mercy's going to make a good stew with some moose we brought."

"Oh, my, you didn't have to."

The familiar courtesies fooled me into relaxing a little. "We're certainly never going to eat it all. Mr. Jefferson must have killed the biggest bull in the county."

A faint smile passed across her face. "Thank you." Her lips formed the words but hardly a sound came out.

My vision blurred and darkened, narrowing to a dim tunnel. I knew I was about to faint. I began creeping toward the door with my hand on the wall. "I think I should get Sadie for you."

"No, no. The cold. She doesn't...."

"Yes, I'll get her."

I couldn't stay for her reply. My legs trembled so badly I almost fell into the kitchen. The change of light seemed to steady me. Mr. Jefferson was kneeling on the hearth cutting kindling. The children were shy again, watching him with round eyes. Mercy sat at the table, still holding the baby, who was sucking his fingers and gurgling.

"We're going to fetch Sadie," I said. "She'll be able to help your mother."

"Thank you, miss," Mercy said.

"I'm sure she'll be all right soon. Sadie will know what
to do." I felt like a fool, running away. I knew that I should
stay, send Mr. Jefferson for Sadie, but I couldn't. Mercy said
nothing as we left the house.

Back in the sleigh, I gulped the snowy air into my lungs as
Mr. Jefferson urged Hazel into motion.

"Is their mother dying?" he asked.

I shuddered, remembering her face. "Probably."

"The girl isn't old enough to take care of the other children
by herself."

"No. There's an aunt in Windsor. Maybe she'll take them
in." I didn't tell him I had helped to birth the baby.

The shushing of the runners and Hazel's harness bells
filled the air for the next mile. My senses gradually returned
to normal and I felt an easy restfulness, sitting beside Mr.
Jefferson. It no longer mattered if he took over the farm.
Maybe Father should sell it to him, I thought. He would take
care of it well, probably far better than I could. I watched the
snowy trees passing and saw no need to fill the space with
words. For the first time, I felt comfortable with him. He
wasn't a stranger anymore.

When we returned to the house, I reported Mrs. Spencer's
condition to Sadie, making sure I skipped the part about my

uncontrolled panic. After a quiet conversation with Father she packed her bag and left. In front of the kitchen fire, after a late supper of moose meat, Father told me that he would arrange for Mrs. Spencer's sister to come from Windsor. By the time she arrived three days later, however, Mrs. Spencer had died. I thought of the children, and of Marie-Madeleine's mother dying before she'd had a chance to see her youngest baby walk, or talk, or sing. At least Marie-Madeleine had her father.

The shortest day passed, and we marked Christmas. The church was barely half full since the weather was so poor. Snow fell, then rain, then more snow.

On the first day of the new year we were invited to the Lovetts' for a party. There was to be music, and supper. I claimed a headache so I could stay at home. Father complained about having to leave the warm fire, but once there, I knew, he would enjoy the food and wine and talk. Mother fussed that her dress was out of fashion and fretted, as usual, that I was missing a valuable social opportunity. One of Mrs. Lovett's nephews was visiting, she informed me. He was rumoured to be an excellent dancer.

By the time they were finally gone, my feigned headache had become quite real. Sadie went to her loom, and I sat at the kitchen table with a cup of tea, rubbing my temples. When I looked up, Mr. Jefferson was standing by the fire.

He coughed once, said, "Miss Evans," then stopped. "Elizabeth," he began again, "I have spoken to your father, and…."

I had learned that he was not a talkative person, but he seemed to be having trouble finding any words at all. He cleared his throat and scratched his neck.

"I have grown very attached to this farm."

"I've noticed." I sat very still, hoping the conversation would be short.

"And to your family, and your father seems to approve of the work I've done. While I was in the woods, waiting for the moose, I—"

For the first time since his dunking in Sawmill Creek, I recognized that he was fumbling, awkward. I might have been amused, if it weren't for the headache. "For heaven's sake, just say it." I wanted to relieve us both of his anxiety.

He hesitated no more. "Your father has agreed to my plan to marry you. We can stay here and the farm will be ours."

I was shocked, and embarrassed, but I suppressed my feelings as quickly as I could. I didn't want him to mistake the flush in my face for pleasure. "I'm not staying here. Didn't you know?" I said the words in a flat, cold voice. "When spring comes, I'm going to Massachusetts, to live with my uncle's family. I'm not staying here."

"I see." His eyes did not meet mine. "I'm sorry to have troubled you." He turned and went up the back stairs to his room.

I felt like I was watching the scene through the window, seeing myself in the chair by the table, and Mr. Jefferson, stone-faced, in his room above me. Then the picture dissolved and I fell back into my body with a disappointing thud. Sadie had been right all along, I thought. I got up from the chair and went upstairs to my own room. When I parted the curtains a few minutes later I saw him striding out across the orchard through the snow. The edge of the sky was a pale pink.

Chapter Thirteen

❧

*O*nce the deep snow had settled in the woods and my
strength had returned to normal, I spent many of January's
cold, clear days on snowshoes. I often passed near the beech
tree, uncertain of whether I hoped for some sign of Marie-
Madeleine. My relief at the sight of the empty tree was
shadowed with guilt. I could picture her gathering firewood
to keep the cabin warm, and cooking whatever meat she
and her father had been able to hunt, but I was unable
to imagine what I could say to her after all this time had
passed. She must think I have abandoned her, I thought,
and I can't face telling her that when spring comes I will do
exactly that.

I told no one about Mr. Jefferson's proposal. Even when
Charlotte came to play the piano, I kept the story to myself.
I knew she would think I was lucky to have an offer, and
ridiculous to say no. Now there, I thought, was a girl who had

undoubtedly dreamed of the moment of proposal many times. I wondered if the real question, when it came, would match her vision.

Mr. Jefferson spent his days cutting logs. He harnessed Hazel every morning and disappeared into the shelter of the woods. One afternoon, I saw him as I came along the edge of the cornfield. His face was red from the wind. I waited beside the track.

"Need a ride?" he called out as he reined in Hazel. It was the most he'd said to me since the new year had begun.

I nodded and climbed onto the sledge to stand beside him as he started Hazel carefully down the hill. I could smell the cut logs behind me.

We crossed the blank expanse of snow-covered field, like an enormous sheet of paper without a single mark on it. I found my mind returning to his proposal. Enough time had passed that I was able to consider it with a little sympathy, mixed with regret. If he had asked a few months earlier, I thought, our situation might be quite different. Would we have made a good match? I remembered his concern over Mrs. Spencer's children, the quiet way he smiled at them as he filled their wood box with dry kindling. He could have been the right father. I shook the thought away, knowing it was useless to pine for what might have been.

I watched the way he held the reins, giving Hazel plenty of slack, always prepared to encourage if she faltered, or check her if she was reckless. I had spent so many weeks seeking his flaws so I could dislike him, and now all I saw were strengths.

At the barn Mr. Jefferson unhitched Hazel and I led her into her stall. He followed and began unbuckling the harness as I broke the skim of ice on the water bucket and forked some hay into the manger.

Mr. Jefferson's voice interrupted the quiet barn sounds. "I think your father is anxious to know how you answered me."

"You haven't told him?" I felt awkward; it hadn't even occurred to me that Father didn't already know.

He shook his head. I watched his reddened fingers struggle with the stiff leather. Then he looked up at me. "What would you tell him, if he were to ask you?"

"I would remind him of the obvious truth. He knows I'm leaving." Hazel struck the floor of her stall with one hoof.

Mr. Jefferson began to brush her, running the bristles smoothly down her neck and over her back. "He didn't know that when we first discussed it."

"And when was that?" I felt my face growing warm. How often had they talked about me? How long had my father known of Mr. Jefferson's intentions and not revealed them to me?

"We were digging potatoes. It must have been late September."

Despite my annoyance, I smiled at the idea of the two men discussing marriage while digging in the dirt. And what was I doing then? I thought, sobering. I was imagining a perfect world in which Marie-Madeleine and I ran a farm together. What a fool I was.

"I assume you made your decision sometime later," Mr. Jefferson said as he opened the barn door and allowed me to go ahead.

"Yes. That's correct." Then a new worry came to me. "And what about my mother? She was still in Sudbury when you first spoke to Father. What does she know about any of this?"

"I don't know."

He followed me along the narrow path cut through the snow between the barn and the house. I turned my head so he would hear me and said, "I'm sure I would have heard about it if Father had told her."

He laughed, and then pretended to cough. I allowed my own smile to stay on my face.

"When you speak to my father," I said, wanting to give him a clear answer, "you should tell him the truth, unless it embarrasses you."

"No," he replied quickly, and then after a pause, "I'm sure he knows that my proposal was meaningless."

We were at the kitchen door as he said it and my hand was on the latch. I looked at him. "No," I said quietly. Whoever was in the kitchen need not hear. "Not meaningless. Impossible, but not meaningless."

A few mornings later when I was milking the cows, Father came into the barn and asked if I had changed my mind about leaving in the spring.

"No. I haven't. Why do you ask?" I kept on milking, listening to the rhythmic sound of the milk spraying the side of the bucket.

"Nothing has happened to make you reconsider?"

"No, Father. There is nothing that could make me reconsider. I thought you understood that." The cow raised a hind foot in irritation at my vigorous tugging. She would soon kick over the bucket if I wasn't more careful.

"I see." Father stood in the middle of the barn floor, fiddling with the buttons on his waistcoat. I thought he looked very much like a small boy at that moment. Finally, he spoke again, with some hesitation. "I thought, perhaps…Mr. Jefferson, you see…."

I stepped in and saved him. "Yes, Mr. Jefferson told me he planned to marry me. And if anyone had been thoughtful

enough to tell him I was going to Massachusetts, he would
have saved his pride and kept his proposal for someone else."

"But Elizabeth—"

"What, Father?" My annoyance had swelled to anger
and I could no longer keep up the pretence of milking.
"You thought that if he asked me to marry him I would just
forget everything and throw myself into his arms and all
would be forgiven? No. I am leaving." I emphasized each
word. "I told Mr. Jefferson that and I remind you of it again.
There is nothing to keep me here. I would have left already
but for the winter weather. Believe me, that is all that holds
me." I turned my face away from him and rested my cheek
against the warm cow. It was difficult to swallow past the
hard place that had formed in my throat, but I refused to
cry.

When he spoke again it was with his softest, most patient
voice. "I thought time might have softened you a little, my
dear. And Mr. Jefferson's proposal might have given you a
chance to start again."

Oh, I thought, why do I have to have the father who
speaks his thoughts with such eloquence and clarity when all
I can do is choke on my own tears? "No," I managed to say.
"No."

"I'm sorry."

After a moment, when I realized he wasn't leaving, my hands returned to their familiar job. I swallowed past the pain in my throat and tried my voice again. "Does Mother know any of this? Did you tell her about Mr. Jefferson's plans?"

"No, I didn't," he said. "And we both know why." Normally we would have laughed together, but when I looked up I could see his sad resignation. The corners of his mouth turned down and his eyes were brimming. A cold draft swirled into the barn as he went out the door.

Lying in bed that night, unable to sleep, I felt the full weight of Father's sadness lying on my chest like a sack of river mud. I considered the condition of his marriage. He was, I felt certain, less than a joyful husband. He tolerated Mother and tried to honour her, but most of the time he simply kept to his own affairs. Aside from their arguments over my life, they hardly seemed to talk to each other. I remembered him saying once that she had been a different woman when she was young. Spirited, he had called her. Was it coming to Annapolis that had diminished her? I didn't want a marriage that turned sour—better to have none at all.

I was sure I heard every creak and mouse scrabble until long past midnight. When sleep finally came, I dreamed I was on a high branch of the beech tree. Marie-Madeleine was a bird perched above me. I was trying to catch her, but she flitted out of reach every time I got close. Then I could feel myself falling.

Before the sky had lightened I was in the kitchen. I startled Sadie as she came grumbling sleepily out of her room.

"Lord, child," she said when she saw me. "You trying to stop my poor heart once and for all?" She put her hand to her chest but her fierce look was half-teasing.

"Sorry, Sadie. I need to talk to you about something."

She put a log on the fire, even though I had built it up sufficiently, then straightened stiffly and looked at me. "How come everybody seems to think I'm such a book of wisdom? I don't know nothin'." Her mock ignorance was an old trick. I knew better.

"You know everything," I said. "And who else has been coming to you for advice lately?"

"Oh, your Mr. Jefferson was bending my ear the other day." She tossed this over her shoulder as she took the cloth off the risen bread dough in its big mixing bowl.

"He certainly is not mine. What did he want?"

"It's between him and me." She put a firm fist into the middle of the soft, puffy dough. It deflated with a sigh.

"Was he talking about me?" I began taking the breakfast dishes from the shelves.

"Betsy, you always did think the world revolved around you. You're supposed to grow out of that notion."

"Sadie."

"I'm not telling." She was busy with the fire again, adjusting the logs to make room for the kettle. I knew that any further coaxing would be a waste of words.

We worked quietly for a while. I set out the breakfast things, and Sadie put the bread in the oven. When she finally sat down, I said, "Do you know why Father's so unhappy?"

"I sure hope you're not looking to me for the answer, 'cause you know very well what's doing it. She's sitting right here." Her voice was sharp with an anger I hadn't heard for years.

I held my tongue.

She went on, shaking a finger. "When a man's only child tells him she doesn't want anything more to do with his home—"

"How did you—" I tried to cut in but she kept right on talking.

"Would break any man's heart."

"That's not what I wanted to do."

"You blamed him for everything you brought on yourself. All he did was make the best possible home for you."

"But, Sadie…"

"But nothing. You've got some nerve to think you can do

whatever pleases little Miss Elizabeth and not care for anyone else. You've been like that your whole life. Same as your mother."

I had been scolded by Sadie countless times before but never had I felt her scorn burn so deep. I sat at the table and buried my face in my apron. For a long time, it seemed, I just sat and cried, until the cloth was soggy. Sadie sat by the fire in her rocking chair, saying nothing. Finally, I stopped sniffling and raised my head. My eyes ached. "I know I've hurt you, too, Sadie. And I'm sorry."

"I'm glad to hear you say that," she said without halting the motion of her chair or taking her eyes off the fire. "But it doesn't make things right. 'Specially not for your father. He loves you more than anything."

As I sat staring into the fire a clear picture of Marie-Madeleine's face formed in my mind. She would never abandon her father. What would she think of me for leaving mine? I knew then that I couldn't leave Annapolis without seeing her again. I had to explain. More than anyone else, I needed Marie-Madeleine to understand.

Chapter Fourteen

❧

The winter dragged on. February brought stronger sunlight and deep blue shadows in the snow. The thick river ice rose and fell as a solid block with every tide, and it mixed with the mud to form an ugly mass, veined with cracks. I continued my solitary pursuits—milking the cows alone, reading alone, walking alone, and waiting for the chance to talk to Marie-Madeleine.

Mother continued to leave me to myself, for the most part. I'm sure my gloominess was more than she could bear, given her own tendency to be low-spirited. I often thought of what Sadie had said to me that dark morning in the kitchen. Was I really so much like my mother? It frightened me to think that I might grow more and more like her as I aged. And living with her family in Massachusetts would only enhance the resemblance. Would leaving Annapolis create the bitter, hard place in my heart that coming here had done for Mother? All these thoughts churned in my mind, preoccupying me.

Charlotte continued her lessons, but they had grown less frequent as the winter passed. One afternoon, after she had played half-heartedly while I sat staring out the window, paying no attention to the music, she spoke her mind.

"Miss Elizabeth," she said, still looking at the pages spread before her, "I do not wish to continue."

"That's fine," I said. "We can leave it for another day." The phrase came without thought. I didn't bother to ask if she was unwell, or unhappy.

"No. I mean, I do not wish to continue." She spoke carefully, slowly.

"You don't want any more lessons?" She had my attention.

"That's correct." She still didn't look at me, but began gathering the music, shuffling the papers with nervous energy.

"Are you sure? What does your father think?"

"I've told him, and he agrees. It's…it's too far from town. There is someone near us who is willing…Father says he may get me a piano of my own. I may not even take lessons anymore." She was still shuffling the pages.

I took them from her and shut them in the cupboard, all in a jumble. "Is that all then?"

She paused, got up and walked across the room, then stopped at the edge of the rug. "No, it's not." She looked at me directly for the first time since she'd arrived. "I wanted us to be friends, Elizabeth. I've tried hard to like you, to see past all your bad manners and your unconventional ways, but over these last few months you have been so…well, so dark, and so absent. I find it very distressing to be with you. So I choose not to. Good day." And with that she walked out of the room.

I listened for the sound of the door shutting firmly behind her, and stayed perfectly still, right where she'd left me, until after she had walked briskly down the lane.

Mother must have seen her leaving. A few minutes later she bustled into the room. "I've decided to go with your father to town this afternoon. He has a long day in court tomorrow and I want to make sure he doesn't exhaust himself. We won't be back for at least two days."

I didn't respond or look up.

She sat down near me. "I know how hard it is for you, Elizabeth, that you don't make friends easily. I was fortunate to have had sisters, growing up. I didn't need to find friends for companionship."

"I can understand why you miss them so much."

"Yes." She smoothed out the cloth of her dress. "But sometimes we have to move on in life, we can't let ourselves be held back by what was important in the past. I came back from Sudbury for the same reason I always come back, because I am your father's wife and he needs my support."

My face, as she spoke, had somehow signalled my disbelief, because she smiled and nodded her head.

"There are many things I cannot do, but I can be here for him, as his mate." She got up and crossed to the door. "You are more like me than I expected, Elizabeth. Be careful that melancholy does not overwhelm you." After she closed the door I heard her calling to Father in her high, excited voice.

The next morning I woke to a brilliant clear sky, clean white snow covering the fields and trees, and sunshine. I knew as soon as I looked out the window that it was no day to stay inside brooding.

I milked the cows and ate a quick breakfast alone. The house was empty. Mr. Jefferson was hauling logs with the Bencrofts, and Sadie had gone to visit a woman who was expecting a child. I packed some bread, cheese, and salt pork in my satchel, put on my snowshoes, and headed away from the house and barn, not knowing where I might go. I just needed to be in the air.

It didn't take long for me to realize that I was headed for the beech tree. Part of me knew there was no chance I would find Marie-Madeleine there that day, or maybe any day, but my heart needed some reminder of what she and I had made together. I climbed the tree and brushed a mound of snow off the branch, watching it fall into the drift below. Then I sat and looked over the smooth, white field and the snow-laden trees. Everything was level, all the bumps and broken places invisible. As if the land could forget all our old mistakes and give us a chance to start again.

I ate my cheese and thought about Marie-Madeleine eating cheese the day she had told me how her family had escaped from the soldiers. This time, when I went over the story in my mind, there were no burning barns, no screams, only Marie-Madeleine's dark hair and eyebrows, her rough hands, her small, neat body. If she and her father had gone to St. Mary's Bay with the others, perhaps a young man in their new village had found her and wanted to make a life with her. Maybe she would have lots of children to make up for her lost brothers and sisters. Maybe she had made her way back to France, to find the place her people had come from so long ago.

When the cheese was gone, and my mind had exhausted itself with wondering, and my legs were sore and cold from the frozen tree, I jumped down into the snow. Before I turned away, an impulse came to me. I tore a strip of blue cloth from the bottom of my skirt, and tied it around the branch. Halfway across the field I turned to see the strip of blue waving in the slight breeze that had come up over the hill. It looked like a flag atop a schooner's mast.

Two days later I set out to check the snares. I took the long route and passed across the field below the beech tree. I could see my blue cloth from that distance, but something else made me stop and stare. It couldn't be, I thought. I ran through the snow, lifting my knees high to keep the snowshoes from catching and tripping me. Breathing hard from the exertion and the sense of anticipation that gripped me, I stopped at the edge of the field and looked up. Sure enough, another flag flew beside my own. No one would...no one else.... My mind raced.

When I reached the tree I touched the second ribbon gently, as if it might disappear in an instant. It was the same rough, brown cloth that I remembered so vividly from Marie-Madeleine's cabin, the blanket she had covered me with as I slept before her fire. I could almost taste the rich brothy stew she had fed me. Then I was tasting salt and knew it was my own tears. She was here. She saw my flag. She made her own. I had never known the rising joy I felt at that moment. Nothing had ever made me so happy.

But now what, I thought. What do I do next? I went to the snares and found two rabbits, then came back to the tree, tied the legs of one rabbit to my blue ribbon and left it hanging.

I would come back every day, even twice a day, I swore, until we found each other.

The next morning, when I returned, the rabbit was gone and a rolled-up piece of hide dangled in its place. It was pale brown and so soft to the touch that I stood for a moment just letting my fingers caress it, knowing Marie-Madeleine's fingers had touched it. When I unrolled it, I found a drawing made with charcoal. It showed a tree, and under the branches, two figures, each with a wide smile. The figures' hands were joined. No words were needed. I rolled the drawing up again and slid it into my pocket in exchange for the molasses I had brought. I hoped it wouldn't be frozen when she got it, just thick and stiff. A little time by the fire would soften it up.

When I arrived home, Father was in the kitchen with Sadie. I could smell turnip, and apples. Father's face was twisted in a grimace.

"What's wrong?" I asked.

"Samuel Bencroft was here...." His voice faded.

The last time he came, I thought, it was because of a bear. What now?

Sadie said it for him. "Mr. Jefferson's been hurt."

"Hurt? Badly?"

"We don't know," Father said. "They're bringing him out of the woods now. I shouldn't have agreed. He doesn't know."

He was mumbling and shaking his head.

A commotion in the yard brought us to our feet. Two large men carried Mr. Jefferson through the door. They deposited him where Sadie pointed—in the room beside the kitchen. A patch of red began growing on the quilt under his head, which was wound around with torn cloths stained the same colour.

"We're mighty sorry," one of the men was saying to Father. "He was doing real good work, just didn't see which way the tree was coming down. Have you got any rum? He's prob'ly gonna need it when he comes to. If…." He stopped talking when the other man elbowed him, and they both turned and went out.

I stood stupidly in the middle of the kitchen watching Sadie go to work. All I could think was how glad I was that she was home. She had begun to unwind the sodden cloth from around his head. I couldn't watch, but tended to the vegetables over the fire.

"Get the biscuits before they burn," Sadie called out, as if she was just spinning in the other room, instead of trying to keep a man's life from slipping away.

By the time she was able to sit and eat some dinner, Sadie had cleaned him up, re-bandaged his head, and tended to his other injuries. His shoulder had been torn out of place and she'd had to enlist Father's help to set it right. Mr. Jefferson had made only one sound through the whole process—a moan that seemed to come from somewhere deep inside his body. It frightened me. He didn't open his eyes.

When Sadie said there was nothing for me to do I left the house on the run, my stomach gnarled in sickening knots and my hands clenched so tight I thought I might never get them loosened. I ran straight for the beech tree, climbed up, and sat shivering on the branch. I hadn't brought enough clothing and the sharp wind seemed to slice through me.

A voice made me jump. "Elizabeth?" The click of the *t* at the end of the name was enough to ease the ache that had begun creeping through my shoulders. Marie-Madeleine climbed up into the tree, with the familiar blanket around her shoulders, and we hugged each other hard, neither wanting to let go first.

She put the old blanket over us both. My shivering slowed and I began to talk. I told her everything that had happened since I'd seen her last—the fever, my decision to leave, Mr. Jefferson's proposal, Sadie's scolding, Charlotte's rejection, and the accident. When I stopped talking, she said nothing, but sat holding my hand between hers.

"I missed you," she said after a long silence.

"Oh, Marie-Madeleine, I'm so sorry, so sorry that I…."

She held up her hand as if to stop my words. I could only smile. But then the weight of everything crashed in on me again and I began to cry.

"You don't want to go away from here. *C'est vrai?*" She looked into my eyes.

"No, I don't," I told her, and the confession felt good. "*C'est vrai.* I thought I did. But I can't. I just can't."

"So. What do you do?"

I had no answer for her or for myself. "But you!" I turned to look into her eyes. "*Comment ça va?*" It wasn't the right question to fill in the months of silence, but it was the best I could do.

She shrugged. "*Je ne sais pas. Mon père…*he is thinking maybe he is too tired. I am worried for him. He has been a strong man all these years. Now I try to be strong for him. But he does not want it. He yells, I yell. We are not so good."

I thought of Father twisting his waistcoat buttons.

"The winter 'as been bad," she went on. "Papa goes to the Mi'kmaq camp and stays with them. I don't see him for two week, maybe."

"You've been alone?"

She looked up through the branches as a few clumps of snow fell to the ground. "He see nothing for his life."

"But what about you? He has you."

She shrugged.

"My father knows about you now," I said quietly. "I told him."

She looked at me with alarm in her eyes.

"No, no," I reassured her. "He's good at keeping secrets. I made him promise. So there's no reason now why you couldn't come home with me."

"But your mother. She doesn't know?"

"You're right, she doesn't. But I don't care anymore. She'll be in a fuss no matter what I do. She doesn't know about Mr. Jefferson's proposal, either. Maybe I'll distract her with that news and she won't even notice you."

She didn't laugh. "No. It would not be good," she said.

"But you're alone."

"I don't mind. I am wanting to be there for my father. He'll come back. I know."

"I wish I could be as sure as you," I said. "I don't think Mr. Jefferson will ever come back to us, and I feel like there is nothing I can do. Sadie knows how to help, but I don't."

"You can wait with him. You can be close by."

We sat together without words for a few minutes, then Marie-Madeleine reached into the folds of her clothing. When she brought her hand out it held the cross I had given her.

"You will need this now," she said, pressing it into my hand. "You say a prayer for Mr. Jefferson, and for my father, too. That can be your work." Then she kissed my cheeks, one after the other. Our visit was over.

As I walked home, the warmth of renewed friendship slowly sceped away when I thought of what was happening at Evans Hall. I had done nothing to help, had abandoned Sadie and Mr. Jefferson when they needed me, all because I was afraid, all because I couldn't bear to acknowledge someone else's pain. I began to quicken my pace, then to run. At the kitchen door I was gasping for breath and ready to do anything, renounce anything, as long as Mr. Jefferson didn't die before I had the chance to make amends.

Chapter Fifteen

Sadie and I took turns through the night, sitting by the bed, watching for any sign of life. The wind howled around the house and seemed to creep in at every corner. When Sadie slept, I kept myself awake by listing the books of the Bible in my head.

In the morning, Mr. Jefferson's eyes were still closed and his face motionless.

"Go to church," Sadie ordered. I hadn't even realized it was Sunday.

I sat between Mother and Father and prayed as I never had before, holding the cross clenched in my fist. After the service, Father said he would take Mother to Lovetts' for the rest of the day. They left me at the bottom of our lane and went on in the sleigh. It had begun to snow, tiny light flakes falling straight to the ground. Walking up the hill between the bare trees I knew it would keep on falling for many hours.

In the kitchen, Sadie was warming some broth. "We need to get something into him, keep his strength up."

"Do you want my help?"

"Bring those bandages. It's time to change his dressing."

I held his head while she unwrapped the length of bloody cloth from around his head. I turned my face away when she peeled off the last piece. I didn't want to see what was underneath. She bathed his wound, and handed me the basin of water when she was finished. I tossed it out the kitchen door, cringing at the sight of the pink drops splattered against the snow.

After she had spooned a little broth into his mouth, Sadie left me in charge while she went to rest. I sat beside the bed, listening to his faint breathing. The snowflakes against the window seemed to make more sound. His coppery hair was almost completely covered by the bandages. His narrow nose, his thin mouth, his bony shoulders, they all looked just the same.

If he dies, I found myself thinking, we might lose the farm after all. He had given so much of himself in such a short time. Looking at his hands resting on the quilt, I realized that if he died something else would be lost. A friendship, a life I valued.

As the afternoon wore on and the snow fell thick and steady, my heavy eyelids stayed closed for longer and longer spells. I must have been fully asleep when a small sound woke me. I felt a surge of nervous energy rush through my limbs and my heart pounded, then gradually quieted. Mr. Jefferson had not moved. A mouse, I thought, or the wind. Snow filled the window's view.

I reached forward to pull the bedclothes up around his shoulders. Just as my hand touched the quilt, Mr. Jefferson opened his eyes. As if he had only blinked, there they were, open. It surprised me so that I gasped.

"Mr. Jefferson," I said, leaning over and holding his arm.

His eyes slid over towards mine and his mouth changed ever so slightly. He had heard me.

"Sadie," I called quietly. "Sadie." No response. "You just wait a minute," I said. "I'll be right back." He still didn't move, but his eyes stayed open, roaming about as if he were trying to find something he recognized. They met mine again. My mind flashed to the day he had arrived at Evans Hall and looked me in the eye. This time I didn't look away. "I'll be right back," I said again.

Sadie was asleep by the fire, sitting in her chair. "Sadie, he's awake!"

"Who?"

"Mr. Jefferson. He's awake!"

"Oh, my soul," she said, pushing herself up out of the chair.

Mr. Jefferson's eyes were closed, but he opened them again as soon as Sadie spoke his name.

"Well, I'll be," she said with a wide grin. "I never thought I'd be talking to you again, sir."

He moved his eyes to meet hers and his mouth made the same small movement, a little more this time. I was amazed that I could have forgotten the colour of his eyes, the bits of light brown that radiated out from the black centre.

By morning the snow had stopped. Between the house and barn a huge drift had formed, like a giant wave. Under its crest the grass was nearly bare, and yet just a few steps away the snow would have been up to my chest. I cut a path to the barn and milked and fed the cows. A little snow had sifted through the cracks around the door, but it would soon melt with the warmth of the animals.

Before dinnertime Father returned from his storm-stayed night at Lovetts'. He was full of concern and wonder at the depth of the snow but when we told him the news he rushed into the patient's room. When he came into the kitchen again, he was shaking his head. "I didn't suppose I would ever see a miracle," he said, "but I think that may be one."

In the days that followed, Mr. Jefferson found his voice and was moving his body more and more, though he was still bedridden. On Father's suggestion I began reading aloud to

the patient. Sadie made sure I included the Bible, Father
suggested history, and I added the Greek myths to the
list, thinking they might be more diverting. Mr. Jefferson
showed no preference but listened with silent attention, and
when I finished each reading, he thanked me and went back
to sleep.

When Mother returned, she found me at Mr. Jefferson's
bedside, reading. She motioned for me to come into the
kitchen. I excused myself, laying the ribbon on the open page
and setting the book on my chair.

"Do you think that's appropriate?" Mother said in a loud
whisper just outside the door.

"What, the story?"

"No," she gestured to the door and lowered her voice
even further. "That you should be alone with this man in his
bedroom."

"For heaven's sake, Mother," I scoffed, unable to hide my
contempt. "If you had been here—" I stopped myself before
saying something hurtful. "He enjoys the reading. That's all."

My answer seemed to satisfy her, and she left me alone.
From then on she avoided the room off the kitchen as if it
contained a plague victim. When Mr. Jefferson began getting
out of bed to sit in front of the kitchen fire, she had Sadie
bring her meals to the sitting room.

"You don't understand, Elizabeth," she said to me one evening. "I used to be as strong and brave as you." I had played a few tunes for her and her mood was gentle. She seemed to be talking to the air, not to me. "I almost died when you were born. The doctor said I could have no more children. That's when I became fearful, and weak. I cannot see blood without the whole room tilting and spinning, and I feel that the floor will open and swallow me up." I didn't know whether to cry or laugh. She had offered me a truth I had never known before, a new window into her sorrow, and my own fears. I leaned over the back of her chair and kissed the top of her head as I made a silent vow to never let panic overcome me again.

I wanted Sadie's ability to heal, not Mother's need to run away. I wanted to be firm in my decisions, but as winter drew to a close, my spirits sank along with the melting snow. Spring would force me to confront what I feared most— saying goodbye. I wasn't ready yet.

On the night of the full moon, a fierce storm blew in over the mountain. I thought the gale might steal the house away. The cows bawled in the barn, tree branches flew across the yard, and the rain pounded against the ground and buildings. When daylight came we looked out to see the marsh covered in water. The dykes had been unable to hold back the storm surge.

"Agh," Father said in disgust. "There goes a crop of hay for this year. The salt will ruin the fields."

"I'm glad I got some of that clearing done," Mr. Jefferson said. He had begun spending much of his time up and about, fixing tools and carving wood. Sadie joked about teaching him to weave. He probably would have given it a good try.

"I still say the dykes are worth fixing," I muttered into my tea.

"Not if there's no way to make the flood gates work properly again." Father was curt.

I said nothing more. There was nothing to be gained by arguing with him. You can't grow crops with feelings, he would say. But I hated the thought of giving up the fields in the marsh. If Mr. Jefferson had worked to build those dykes, I said to myself as I stared out at the dismal scene, he would certainly be fighting to preserve them.

Chapter Sixteen

The next afternoon, under the meagre shadows of the beech tree's bare branches, I told Marie-Madeleine about the flood. We both sat with our faces turned to the spring sunlight.

"Ah, *oui*, I saw. Water all over."

"And now Mr. Jefferson will convince Father that the marshland isn't worth saving."

"*Mais le pré, c'est le meilleur!*"

"*Le pré?*"

She pointed. "The marsh, you call it. The fields. My father says they are the best land for growing. He was talking always about 'ow the men would go out in the spring to build up the broken dyke and fix *les aboiteaux*."

I didn't know what that word meant but it didn't matter. I seized her arm. "Your father!" I yelled.

"*Oui, mon père.* What of him?"

"Your father. Of course!" I was so excited I nearly knocked us both off the branch.

She still looked baffled. "Those are not his fields."

"But my father and Mr. Jefferson are willing to leave them flooded just because they don't know how to fix them. The *aboiteaux*, that's what you said?"

"*Oui. Mais, c'est fou.*" She was shaking her head. I could tell she was beginning to understand my idea.

I jumped down, too impatient to explain all the reasons why it had to work. "Come back tomorrow, as early as you can!" I called over my shoulder as I ran off down the hill, leaving Marie-Madeleine sitting on the branch.

When I burst into the kitchen, Mr. Jefferson and Sadie looked up with alarm in their faces.

"I know how the dykes can get fixed," I said, out of breath and still excited.

They both stared at me as if I was speaking an incomprehensible language.

"The dykes," I repeated, pausing to slow my breathing. "I know someone who used to farm out there, who used to help repair those very dykes every spring before we were even here."

"Does your father know about this?" Sadie asked. She held her flour-covered hands over the bowl of bread dough.

I grabbed Mr. Jefferson by the arm and pulled him along the hall to Father's study. "Come on, we'll tell him," I said, and without knocking, I burst in and blurted the whole thing out in a rush of words.

"Oh, Elizabeth," Father said in a slow and ponderous voice. "I don't know. It's…it's…."

"It's what?" I demanded. "How could this not be good for everyone?" I didn't understand why no one else could see it as clearly as I did.

"I don't think it's worth the trouble," Mr. Jefferson said, his words abrupt and hard. "What else grows out there but hay? And there is plenty of good upland—"

"Oh, you and your upland," I blurted, stamping my foot. "People have been growing crops out there for generations. It's beautiful soil. There are no trees to cut down and it's easy to till because it's flat. What could be better?" I was sure I had an argument that would convince even a stubborn Yorkshire farmer.

Father tried to steer us toward a compromise. "Elizabeth, I know you're very enthusiastic about this idea and I'm happy to see that, but I think we need more information. What if we had a chance to meet this man, to hear for ourselves what he has to say?"

"I could arrange a meeting," I said, without giving myself a chance to think about the idea of my father and Marie-

Madeleine's father in the same room. "It would have to be someplace where he would feel safe," I added. "Not here, not in town. Someplace safe." I considered half a dozen possibilities before the right one came to me. "The bridge," I said. "You can meet him at the bridge over Sawmill Creek. And Marie-Madeleine, too, so she can help you understand each other."

"Well, then, you might as well come, too," Father said. "After all, it is your idea."

Marie-Madeleine, when I told her the plan at the tree the next morning, was even more doubtful than Father had been. "I do not think he will go," she said, shaking her head.

"Just try, please," I pleaded. "You'll be with him, and I'll be there. And we promise that no one will try to harm him in any way. Tell him that. And don't forget," I added, "none of us know where your cabin is. After all this time, even I don't know."

She smiled, a mischievous smile that wiped away her sadness for a moment. We agreed that the meeting would be at the bridge, in three days. That might give her enough time, I thought.

On the appointed day, Mr. Jefferson, Father, and I walked down the muddy road to Sawmill Creek. I was so nervous my hands shook. I held them wrapped tightly in the corners of my shawl. On the bridge, we waited for a long time, not talking. I watched the creek, almost as full of water as it had been when Sadie and I had crossed to Mrs. Spencer's in the dark, a whole year ago.

Finally, we saw someone coming along the path by the river. She walked with her head down, alone.

"I knew it," Mr. Jefferson said, pressing his lips together. Father was silent.

"I'm sorry," Marie-Madeleine said to me when she reached us. She couldn't bring herself to look at the men. I took her aside and, with a heavy heart, asked what happened.

"He just was not happy with this. How can you blame him, eh?" She sounded closer to angry than I'd ever heard her. I knew she was right; I couldn't blame him. She took a deep breath and spoke again. "I think it's a good idea. But my father is too…too nervous. Maybe…."

"What?" I asked, ready to try anything. "Maybe what?"

"A little more time?"

"Oh, time, time. That's what everyone says. How much time? Until after it's too late to save the dykes, until all the soil is so full of salt that nothing will ever grow and the river takes the fields again? No. I cannot do that." I turned away quickly, feeling disappointment and bitterness rising in my throat. I heard Father calling to me to wait, but I went on without them, walking hard all the way home. I ran straight into the barn and buried myself in the last of the old, dusty hay.

Why am I even bothering? I asked myself. Mother was already packing trunks and trying to make me decide which of my belongings I would take and which I would leave behind. I lay in the hay for a long time, thinking about all that had happened over the winter, about what spring would look like on the farm, about how I would feel as a member of Uncle William's household.

It was long past dinnertime when I could stand the hunger pains and the itchiness no longer. I went to the house. I was glad to see that Sadie was the only one in the kitchen. She put a plate of food on the table and I ate in silence.

"Sadie," I said as I pushed the empty plate away. "When Mrs. Spencer died, did you feel helpless?"

"No." She started sweeping the floor around the table where crumbs from my meal had fallen. "I helped her die. That's what she needed."

"But you didn't kill her!" I was shocked at this notion.

The broom stopped. "Of course I didn't. Mrs. Spencer was going to die anyway. I just made it easier for her. More peaceful."

"Oh."

She went back to her sweeping. The only sound in the room was the steady rhythm of the broom against the floor.

"Sadie, are you happy about going back to Massachusetts?"

"Oh, Betsy." She leaned the broom against the wall and sat down at the table, letting out a long sigh. "I'm a tired old woman."

"You're not old." I looked at her greying hair, her wrinkled hands, her stooped back.

"Yes, I am. Old. And much as I love you, the thought of making that trip, and going back to work for your mother's people, well, happy isn't the word I'd use. But you and your mother say we're going, so I'll go." She reached across the table and patted my hand, then got up and went into her room.

I looked at the kettle hanging in the fireplace, at the gun over the mantel, at the grain of the table's wood, the long straight floorboards, the shelves and dishes. I walked into the hall, hearing the murmur of voices. Mother was alone in the sitting room, reading. I put my ear to Father's study door. He and Mr. Jefferson were inside, their voices low. I knocked and pushed the door open.

"Elizabeth," they said together. Mr. Jefferson stood up.

I looked directly at him, seeing again the light brown eyes that I had watched after his accident. "I need to speak to

Robert alone, please." I spoke without taking my eyes from his.

Father didn't hesitate. "I could use some tea," he said quietly, shutting the door on his way out.

I took a deep breath. My hands had started to tremble again. Mr. Jefferson remained standing.

"Do you remember when you asked me to marry you?" I began.

He nodded.

"Well, you didn't actually ask. You said that my father had agreed, but you didn't ask for my agreement."

He looked down at the floor. "I apologize."

"I should apologize. I was rude to you. Even cruel perhaps. You did not deserve it." I went on, leaving him no space to speak. "I know now that I cannot leave this place. It is where I belong. I am going to stay, and I'm going to take over the farm, and I'm going to make it as big as Father ever dreamed." I paused, out of breath and words.

His head came up. He waited, not speaking, not smiling.

"I'm still not sure I need a husband for that, but I know I can't do it alone."

I could swear his eyes got brighter.

I found the courage to go on. "Marie-Madeleine's father will be hired to teach all of us how to repair and tend the dykes. And we will give Marie-Madeleine and her father free access to a piece of our land, to live on, farm, hunt, whatever they wish. And until she and her father can build themselves a proper house, Marie-Madeleine will live here, at Evans Hall. And then I will consider being your wife."

There was a silence in the room that I thought would last forever. He stared at me, seeming to search my eyes. Perhaps he thought I was teasing him. I held his gaze, willing him to recognize my sincerity.

"I agree to your conditions," he said, and reached out his hand. I took it in mine, and we shook firmly.

"We'd better tell my father."

"And your mother, too," he said, with a quick grin.

"And Sadie," I added, before the grin was gone.

Chapter Seventeen

❧

I watched for her all morning and finally, after dinner, I spotted the tiny figure making her way down the very path I had followed on the day we met. She wore her new white cap, and a blue shawl over her shoulders, and she carried a basket in one hand and a satchel in the other.

I found it hard to believe that she really was coming to live with us. Perhaps I had never been completely convinced that my bold plan would work. But there was Marie-Madeleine, coming around the back of the garden and along beside the barn, proving that some things can turn out the way you hope they might.

I met her in the yard. Her face betrayed her own doubts. I beckoned with my finger, hooked my arm in hers, and walked with her around to the front of the house. We stood for a moment taking in the view of pink and white blossoms in the orchard, and beyond to the greening marsh where tiny men moved with oxen and carts, busy with the beginnings of their undertaking.

Then we turned to face the front of the house. I felt Marie-Madeleine draw in her breath and when I looked at her I could see, through her eyes, the true loveliness of it all.

"You are an important guest," I told her. "After today, you can use the kitchen door, like the rest of us."

She smiled at that, and together we marched up the stone steps and through the doors into the hall with the spring sun shining in behind us and all of the possibilities of a new beginning ahead.

Evans Hall, Annapolis
March 1794

My own Abigail,

If you are reading this letter, it means you have come to the
end of the book and found it there, pressed between the last
page and the cover. I know you think it's silly of me to write
you letters when you live so close by, but this is a special time,
so I set aside the ordinary ways.

You now know my version of the events that happened the
year I turned eighteen. Of course, you already knew what was
to come, that I married Robert Jefferson in the summer, that
you were born in March of the next year. And now you have
nine brothers and sisters, with more to come, perhaps. I did
say I would make the farm grow!

Marie-Madeleine stayed with us for a year. She was here
when you were born; she helped Sadie bring you into the
world. And then, in the early summer, she and her father
went to St. Mary's Bay to find their family. You were only two
when we visited her. She took us out into the bay in her boat
and you cried.

As you read, you may be holding your own first-born. I will probably be here in the kitchen, watching your grandfather bouncing your youngest sister on his knee. And maybe your father is just coming in for dinner, washing his hands under the new pump in the kitchen, smiling at the bedlam all around him. He never seems daunted by our life's constant change. I hope you have inherited that quality of his. From me, you probably get your love of cows, and snow.

I am sure I will see you coming up the lane tomorrow, or the next day, through the rows of apple trees. Until then, be well.

Your loving mother,

Elizabeth Jefferson